Susan Carlisle's love affair with books began in the sixth grade, when she made a bad grade in mathematics. Not allowed to watch TV until she'd brought the grade up, Susan filled her time with books. She turned her love of reading into a passion for writing, and now has over ten Medical Romances published through Mills & Boon. She writes about hot, sexy docs and the strong women who captivate them. Visit SusanCarlisle.com.

Also by Susan Carlisle

His Best Friend's Baby
One Night Before Christmas
Married for the Boss's Baby
White Wedding for a Southern Belle
The Doctor's Sleigh Bell Proposal
The Surgeon's Cinderella
Stolen Kisses with Her Boss
Christmas with the Best Man
Redeeming the Rebel Doc
The Brooding Surgeon's Baby Bombshell

A DADDY
SENT BY SANTA

SUSAN CARLISLE

MILLS & BOON

Published in Great Britain 2018
by Mills & Boon, an imprint of HarperCollins*Publishers*
1 London Bridge Street, London, SE1 9GF

© 2018 Susan Carlisle

 ISBN: 978-0-263-07728-5

 MIX
Paper from
responsible sources
FSC **FSC® C007454**
www.fsc.org

This book is produced from independently certified FSC™ paper
to ensure responsible forest management.
For more information visit www.harpercollins.co.uk/green.

Printed and bound in Great Britain
by CPI Group (UK) Ltd, Croydon, CR0 4YY

To Katie

CHAPTER ONE

Paxton Samuels' decision to leave Boston had been calculated. Volunteering for the temporary medical position in western Oklahoma hadn't given him pause. It was his ticket out of the emotional nightmare his life had become. He needed this change in scenery, some privacy. Desperately.

With his experience and training in emergency care and family practice, the temp job was a perfect fit for him. That it was halfway across the country from Boston only added to its appeal. Still, he'd not anticipated driving through a blizzard at the end of November in the middle of nowhere. He'd been prepared for culture shock but not this blowing snow and endless road. The unexpected brutal weather notwithstanding, the move was well worth the effort. It got him away from his parents' demands as well as the media's fascination with the spectacular failure of his wedding, which had been hailed as the "social event of the year."

He searched the empty white plain for any sign of civilization but only spotted an occasional tree. According to his GPS, Last Stop, Oklahoma, should only be a few miles ahead. Visibility was becoming so bad he had thoughts of pulling over until it improved. Still, he couldn't shake the worry that if he did so the rapid snow accumulation would strand him. He had to push on.

Moments later the terrain rose enough to obscure the road ahead. Paxton topped the small rise and instinctively stomped on the brakes. The back end of his sports car fishtailed. He yanked his foot off the brake, steering the car into the spin, and the vehicle straightened. In control again, he slowed to a stop and surveyed the wreckage before him. Blocking the road was a huge combine tractor lying on its side, a truck smashed against it.

His job as local doctor was starting sooner than he'd thought.

Paxton parked on what he guessed was road, making sure two of his tires remained on the pavement. Locating his cell phone, he called 911. The dispatcher answered and he reported the wreck, its location and that he was a doctor.

"Help is on the way," the dispatcher said, and ended the call.

Opening the door, Paxton shuddered at the bone-cutting blast of wind and snow that assaulted him. He snatched his heavy wool overcoat from the front passenger seat and jerked it on. Reaching in again, he pulled out his medical bag. Pushing the door closed with his hip, he shoved his empty hand into a coat pocket and lowered his head against a biting gust. His toes curled in his shoes in an effort to generate heat as he trudged toward the accident.

Reaching the pickup truck, he skidded across a patch of black ice, doing a little twist and turn, before he smacked his hand against the truck to catch himself. When his feet were firmly beneath him, he worked his way to the cab and peered through the driver's side window.

The man inside was slumped forward, his head against the wheel. Paxton knocked on the glass. The man moved slightly but didn't straighten. Grabbing the door handle, Paxton pulled it open and touched the man's shoulder. In a firm but caring tone he asked, "Hey, are you okay?"

The man moaned and attempted to sit up.

"Easy." Paxton gripped his shoulder to hold him in place. "Don't move. I'm a doctor. Can you tell me where you're hurt?"

"My head."

"I want you to remain still."

Swiftly Paxton assessed his head injury. Delving into his open bag and pulling out a packaged four-by-four bandage, he tore it free of the wrapper and pressed it over the man's bleeding gash.

"Someone will soon be here to help you. I need to check on the other person."

The man muttered, "Okay."

Making his way to the overturned tractor, Paxton stabilized himself by pressing a hand on the side of the truck. The cold metal felt like sharp pins beneath his fingers but fear of falling overrode the pain. What light he had was disappearing fast.

At the tractor cab, he rubbed his hand in a circle across the window. From what he could make out there was one young man lying on his side, not moving. Paxton would have to climb up onto the side of the cab of the hulking piece of machinery, then lower himself inside to properly assess the unconscious man's injuries. He studied the tractor. It wouldn't be easy.

Strapping his medical bag over his shoulders, thankful for the growing wail of an approaching siren, he carefully made his way around to the exposed undercarriage. To get inside he'd have to open the cab door. He examined the bottom workings of the engine for a footing. No help there. Even if he could find something to stand on he still couldn't swing high enough to grasp the cab handle. The metal step to the cab was just above his head but not large enough to do him any good. On his best day he couldn't pull himself up within reach of the door.

He looked at the front tire of the tractor suspended in the air. That was his way in. Using the inside rim of the tire for foot support, he hefted himself up on the exposed axle then onto the side of the engine hood. Crawling on hands and knees, he located the latch. At least the engine was still warm enough to give his hands some relief.

Reaching the door, Paxton kneaded his fingers to get them flexible then tried the handle. At first it wouldn't budge. Using his palm, he hit it. His teeth clamped together as pain shot through his arm. After one more knock the handle shifted and he swung the door back. Warmth greeted him but soon vanished into the frigid twilight.

He looked down at a teen, who still hadn't moved. "Hey! Are you okay?"

No answer.

The siren grew louder. Relief washed through him. There would be help soon. In Boston he didn't get tractor accidents so this was a new one for him.

Getting on his belly, Paxton leaned in from his waist until he could touch the closest part of the boy's body, which was his thigh. There was still heat there. He was alive. Carefully Paxton pulled himself back. He didn't need to fall in and cause more damage to the boy or to himself. Sitting on his butt so he could go in feet first, he braced one foot on the side of the seat's backrest and the other on the dash. Leaning as far forward as possible, Paxton just managed to put two fingers on the teen's pulse point just below his jaw. It was faint. If the boy was going to live he needed help soon.

The siren stopped. The strobe of the lights reflected off the cab. Help was finally here.

Pulling his bag strap up over his head, he placed his medical duffel on top of the backrest and against the cab window behind his patient so it wouldn't slide out of his reach. He opened it and one-handedly found his stethoscope. Getting it into his ears, he placed the bell on the teen's chest. A thrill went through him. A heartbeat was there.

As Paxton was reaching for the boy's head a voice snapped, "Don't touch him!"

Looking back over his shoulder, all he could see was a face surrounded by a white cap trimmed in white fur. Echoing that command were rosy lips pulled tight, a small flared nose and wide glaring dark eyes.

"Don't move him!" Lauren Wilson hung over the edge of the cab, using the tone of voice she'd perfected to stop her two-year-old son from doing something that could harm him.

She couldn't have some good Samaritan making matters worse. The situation was bad enough as it was. Her attention zeroed in on the stethoscope the man held. Amazement rocked her. It couldn't be. Luck was with her.

"You wouldn't happen to be Dr. Samuels, would you?"

"I am, and I'm glad to see you. Do you have help coming?"

"I'm your help. Name's Lauren." He didn't look too impressed. "I also have Rick with me. He's a police officer," she added.

"We've got to get this boy and the other man—" he nodded toward the truck "—taken care of. Where's the ambulance? This fellow needs to be gotten out of here and on his way to the hospital."

This wasn't the type of doctor she'd been expecting. Someone older, less attractive. With graying hair and narrower shoulders. There wasn't enough light to tell if his eyes were light blue or green.

Last Stop's longtime physician, Dr. Barden, had retired after forty-five years of service. He'd given up on finding a permanent replacement and had settled for coaxing doctors to at least fill in for a few months at a time, yet often there were no volunteers. The town and neighboring area needed a full-time doctor in residence. Lauren was the only nurse and medical professional for sixty miles. She helped where she could during emergencies until assistance arrived, but the town deserved more. Emergency medical aid was too far away in the absence of EMTs or a resident physician.

Lauren looked over the top of Dr. Samuels as his

attention returned to the patient. She had no doubt he was just one younger doctor meeting his medical school loan requirements. He would soon be gone. But for now she was glad to have him and tonight in particular.

Lewis Williams, the teen who was folded against the cab windshield, she'd known all her life. From the looks of him Dr. Samuels was right. They needed to get him to the hospital right away. "Rick," she called down, "it's Lewis Williams. We need to get him out of here. We're going to need lights, blankets, possibly a rope and your help up here. Throw me my bag." She grabbed it as it sailed through the air. Lauren looked down at Dr. Samuels, who was wearing an expensive-looking coat and no head covering. "We need to get his neck stabilized before we move him."

"I realize that, but I don't have a neck brace with me."

"I have one." She pulled her bag closer. Unzipping it, she reached for the neck ring and handed it to him. He was already working his way around the steering wheel and farther into the cab when she said, "Hold on a minute. I'll climb in and help you."

The confining space would be difficult for two to maneuver in but it would take both of them to get the neck brace into place. Fear clutched at her chest as she eased her way inside.

Young Lewis had just earned a university scholarship. His future was bright. Now this. He reminded her too much of her husband. Young, smart and willing to work hard for what he wanted. Then to have it all destroyed by an explosion. She was brought out of her morbid thoughts by the doctor.

"I want you to support him while I check his head wound. We don't need to make any sudden movements that could make matters worse."

He seemed to be talking to himself as well as her.

"The light is going. And this weather…" He glanced up.

She watched snowflakes settle on his cheeks and forehead. Even in the dimming light, she registered he wasn't the average man in looks or attitude. The few single young women in the area would be fighting over him. He was still speaking and she forced her wandering attention back to the crisis at hand.

"If we don't get him out of here we're gonna have to worry about hypothermia on top of all his other injuries. What's the ETA on the ambulance?"

"Under an hour from the time it was called."

He muttered an expletive as his head jerked around. "That long!"

"The closest hospital is over sixty miles away. In this weather…" She hadn't meant it to sound so harsh, yet it was the truth.

His mouth dropped in disbelief, although whether it was because of the distance or her snapping, she wasn't sure. It might have been comical in any other situation.

His expression went from resigned to determined as he turned back to their patient. "We've got to try and shorten that time or this boy may not make it."

Terror shot through her. Not another wasted life. She couldn't stand another one of those.

He commanded, "Hand me that brace."

She did so then placed a foot on the side of the seat to support herself as she climbed down farther into the cab. By the time she'd gotten situated, he was working the brace around Lewis's neck with one hand while supporting himself with the other against the cab roof. Using her free hand, she helped him get it into place then secured it.

"Good. Now I want to have a look at his head. At least get a four-by-four over the wound. Can you get your arm around his shoulders and pull him toward you while I lift his head?"

The action would put her in an awkward position, but she would try. Lauren nodded. "Hold on a sec." She reached into her bag and pulled out a square paper package, put it between her teeth and tore it open then handed the gauze to him.

Moving her foot on the seat to the floor, which put her in contact with the doctor from hip to foot with the steering wheel column between them, she was stable enough to reach both arms around Lewis and pull him against her chest.

At the same time the doctor used his hands to support Lewis's head. "Good." A second later he said, "It looks like he's taken a good shot to the temple. I'm concerned about his brain swelling. He's still not regained consciousness. You got a blanket in your bag of tricks?"

Just as he said that Rick called, "Lauren, catch." A blanket fell into the cab. She passed it to the doctor as another hit her on the head.

"Rick, we're going to need the rope and you up here," she called.

"What're you thinking?" Dr. Samuels asked as he tucked the blankets around Lewis.

"Tie the rope under his arms and have Rick pull him out as we push and steady him."

"Sounds like a plan. He needs to be in a warmer place than this. I need to check for any broken bones."

"Lauren, here you go," Rick yelled from above them as he lowered an end of rope to them. "Just got a message the ambulance is still twenty minutes out."

Dr. Samuels uttered another word under his breath that she wouldn't want her two-year-old to hear, or repeat.

She announced, "Rick, it's going to take us a few minutes to get Lewis secured, then on my word I want you to pull. We'll help from down here."

Seconds later Rick was holding his flashlight over them.

"As I lift can you get the rope in position?" Lauren asked Dr. Samuels as she wrapped her arms around Lewis once more.

"Yeah." The doctor wound the rope around Lewis and tied it off.

"I'm going up to the door to make sure he doesn't topple over the side as we pull him out." She started her climb, but her foot slipped. She fell against Dr. Samuels. His body was hard and his strong hands grabbed her at the waist. "Sorry," she muttered.

"You get a handhold and I'll help you out," he ground out.

Once she was on the engine hood, Lauren remained on her stomach, twisted around and grabbed the rope. Rick laid the flashlight down and stationed himself behind her. "Okay, on three. One, two, three."

Lauren wrapped her hands around the rope. She pulled with all her might until her muscles burned with the effort. Between her and Rick pulling and Dr. Samuels pushing, Lewis's head came over the door edge then his shoulders.

"Wait. Hold him steady. Let me get hold of him." Using her legs, she dragged Lewis while Rick pulled and the doctor lifted. Lauren kept working until Lewis almost lay across her, his back to her front.

Rick hurried to help her. With Lewis on the engine hood, they rolled him on his side, placed a blanket beside him, and gently positioned him on it before bundling him up and tucking it around him. Cracking all the heating picks she had, she placed them along his side then put another blanket around him. Now they had the chore of lowering him to the ground.

Dr. Samuels, with his bag across his shoulders, hoisted himself out of the cab. He must be freezing in his less-than-suitable clothes, but she hadn't heard a complaint or seen a wince.

With Lewis wrapped burrito-style, she grabbed the rope and tied it around his thighs and shoulders. They couldn't have Lewis slipping out of control.

"This isn't the first time you've done this," Dr. Samuels observed from behind her.

"No." She didn't slow to look at him. "Rick, you ready?"

"Ready."

The doctor grabbed the rope. "What do I need to do?"

In the dim light provided by Rick's flashlight and the running police cruiser headlights she could see Dr. Samuels' fingers were turning dark. He would need attention as well. But that would have to wait until Lewis was taken care of. "We need to keep the rope taut between us as we lower him so that he remains as level as possible."

He nodded.

"On three. One, two, *three*."

Slowly they lowered Lewis a couple of feet to Rick's waiting hands. Minutes later Lewis was on the ground and she was climbing off the tractor. She had just reached the pavement when she was bumped. The doctor had slipped. Seconds later they were sprawling entangled in the snow.

He was the first to recover. His arms were around her and his face close. "I'm sorry. Are you hurt?"

She blinked. "No."

"Good." He scrambled to his feet.

Lauren followed his lead.

"We need to get Lewis out of the elements and see where that ambulance is." He hurried toward Rick, who was untying Lewis.

"I have the cruiser running so it's warm. The back seat is clear," Rick informed them.

As he and Rick carried Lewis around the back of the tractor to the waiting car, Lauren rushed to the far side of the vehicle. Opening the door, she climbed in as Rick laid Lewis's shoulders on the seat. She placed her arms under Lewis's armpits and pulled him toward her. As she did so Dr. Samuels helped by pushing from his end. She kept going until the boy lay across the seat. Before she could straighten up, the doctor joined her on her side.

"Let's get a set of vitals on him," he said with authority. "Rick, could you see to the guy in the truck? The best I could tell, he just has a head wound. I'm not sure how serious. Also, check the ETA on the ambulance."

The doctor was good with issuing orders, but he had stood back when she'd been the one giving them earlier. Hadn't arrogantly assumed command of the situation as other male doctors might have done. She appreciated his unspoken acceptance of her as his professional equal.

Lauren went to the other door, leaving him room to work. Putting down her bag, she removed her stethoscope and blood-pressure cuff. Lewis was so thin there was a chance she could get a reading from his calf. She didn't want to remove the blankets or his jacket unless absolutely necessary. Instead she pushed at Lewis's pants leg in an effort to get it beyond his boot top. Succeeding, she placed the cuff around his leg. With relief, she found it just fit.

"His heart rate is erratic. It wasn't when I first checked," Dr. Samuels said. "BP?"

"One forty-three over one hundred and two."

He shook his head. "We've got to get him to a hospital. We don't have time to waste. Can you get a temp while I check on Rick?"

"Yes."

He disappeared into the night through the blinding snow.

Finding the thermometer, she closed the door to keep the heat in and carefully moved around to Lewis's head and ran the electronic instrument over his forehead. Ninety-six. The acid taste of panic filled her. Lewis was well on his way to hypothermia. With a grateful heart and elation knowing no bounds, she saw the lights of the ambulance arriving.

Dr. Samuels came up behind her. "Go help Rick get the other man here while I report to the EMTs. I may need to ride in with Lewis."

Lauren didn't miss the concern in his voice or him blowing on his cupped hands. He was in pain as well was her guess. Would he shorten his stay in Last Stop after this adventure?

Paxton couldn't remember the last time, or if there had ever been one, he'd done this much physical activity during patient care. He worked out regularly, but he was going to feel tonight's exertions in the morning when he tried to get out of bed.

The lights of the ambulance had been a happy sight. Rick was helping the other man out of the truck when he left to meet the EMTs. He feared Lewis was going to end up having just as many issues from the prolonged exposure to the elements as he did from the actual accident.

When the first EMT approached, he introduced himself and gave a quick report of his examination of the man in the truck, then went into detail about Lewis's care. The second EMT hurried to them with the gurney. Paxton went around to Lewis's feet and crawled across the seat as the other two men worked Lewis's shoulders onto the gurney. Minutes later they had him strapped down. Rick joined them, helping the EMTs get Lewis into the ambulance. As soon as the EMTs had Lewis secured inside, they immediately started working on him. Paxton was told he couldn't ride in the ambulance. He responded, "Then I'll see you at the hospital."

He watched the ambulance leave and returned to

the cruiser to check on his other patient. Lauren and Rick had sat him in the back seat. "I'm going to follow the ambulance in my car," he told her.

"No, you're not," Lauren said in a firm voice that reminded him of his mother refusing him a cookie before dinner when he'd been a child. "I'm going to see about your hands after I get through with Mr. Thompson here. We've got to take him to the hospital as well, so Rick is driving."

"I'll call someone to come get your car. Are the keys in it?" Rick asked.

"Yes." Paxton just experienced another element of culture shock. He'd never have left his keys in his car in Boston, even if he'd been the first medical person on the scene of a bad accident.

"Now get in the back seat," Lauren ordered. "I need to have a look at your hands. You probably have the beginnings of frostbite. Are they numb?"

He had no choice but to admit, "Yeah, they are."

"Let me see." She grabbed a flashlight and shone it on his hands. "Ooh, the tips are already turning white. You should've been wearing gloves."

"I have some in my suitcase but didn't take the time to find them."

"Next time you need to." She pulled off her gloves and stuffed them in a pocket of her coat before reaching for his hands. "Bend them for me."

He started to argue but with the way he felt and her tone of voice he thought better of it. Doing as she instructed, he was disappointed to find his fingers wouldn't move. She was right, he had all the signs of frostbite.

To be ordered around by someone other than his

parents was a new experience. Now that the adrena-line rush was over he was starting to register intense pain. He'd overextended his body in addition to his exposure to the increasingly frigid temperature.

He watched as she turned his hands one way then the other. Her fingers were strong and sure, yet tender. She'd pushed back her coat hood. Snowflakes hung like stars in the night sky in her thick dark hair. Even in the shadowy light he could tell she was pretty in a natural, wholesome way.

"You might as well do as she says because you won't win," the injured man leaned out to say.

"He's right. Get in. We need to get going. I'll work on your hands in the car," Lauren said.

Paxton climbed in next to the man, welcoming the warmth inside despite the still-open door. He attempted to kick off his shoes, but pain shot up his leg. His toes hurt but with the car heat on they would recover soon.

"Let's go, Rick," Lauren called to the policeman, who was doing something near the tractor. She closed the door and headed to the other side of the car.

Somehow the sound of her soft, slow drawl and un-usual tone that could only be native to the region took his mind off his pain. Who was this young woman who lived out in the middle of nowhere? And why did she? After Gabriella's mistreatment of him, he was surprised that he'd even wonder about a woman, but curiosity about Lauren did keep his mind off his discomfort.

Lauren got into the front passenger seat and closed the door. She swiveled in her seat and said, "Give me your hands."

"Again?"

"Yeah. I need to start warming them. You are familiar with frostbite care?" she asked, a little irritated note in her voice.

"Of course I am."

"Then you know I need to bring the feeling back slowly. I don't have any more heat packs so I'll need to hold them between mine. Body heat is the best."

He glanced at the man next to him to see his reaction, but he had his head back and his eyes closed. In a few minutes Paxton would rouse him to make sure he wasn't unconscious from a concussion, but first...

Paxton extended his hands.

Lauren took them between her smaller ones and held them but instead of rubbing movements she blew on them. Her gaze met his, held. Her eyes were as black as the sky he'd so often lain under in Africa. Unspoiled, huge and comforting. There was look of caring he'd not seen in a woman's eyes in a long time. Was he destined to judge every woman by Gabriella? He hoped not. Lauren blinked and the moment was gone.

"You were good out there," he said with true admiration.

"Thanks." She looked pleased with the compliment. Did she not get many of them?

"You know, I'm used to being the one who gives the orders." He watched a slow smile light up her face.

"I know. I heard a few of them tonight."

"I think you're pretty good at them as well." He knew his grin was more grimace than smile.

Rick climbed into the driver's seat. "Everyone ready?"

"Where're we headed?" Paxton asked when they were riding down the road.

"Lippscomb, Oklahoma. Closest hospital. By the way, I'm Lauren Wilson." She nodded to the driver. "This is Rick Moore. That's Art Thompson beside you."

"And I'm Dr. Paxton Samuels. Feel free to call me Paxton."

"You're our new temporary doctor. Tough way to start your month," she said, giving him a reassuring smile.

"I won't argue with that." But everything about the last few weeks had been tough as well.

She continued to blow and after a few minutes she looked at him. "I forgot to mention that I'm your nurse. So this probably won't be our last adventure together."

He wasn't sure if that sounded ominous or inviting, but it was definitely intriguing.

CHAPTER TWO

Lauren blinked at the bright light coming from the hospital emergency department entrance. The ride hadn't been the worst one of her life but it had been uncomfortable. She'd spent most of it with her body twisted toward the back and her arms between the seats, holding Paxton's hands while she blew on them.

They were strong, capable hands. She had already learned that. His fingers were long and tapered down to well-manicured nails. They weren't as soft as she'd expected. Something about them made her think of security. That he could take care of himself and anyone else he cared about.

As they'd driven she'd seen him studying her, his face faintly lit by the dashboard lights. Tingles of self-awareness had flickered through her, as though she were a specimen under a microscope. She feared he was analyzing her both in appearance and intelligence, and passing judgment. Did she fall short or measure up?

They were to the outskirts of Lippscomb before he said, "You can stop. I have feeling now."

"That's good but you're not out of the woods yet. You'll still require medical attention to make sure there hasn't been further damage." She struggled to conceal her relief. Her back hurt and she had become ever more aware of him as a man the longer she'd held his hands.

More disturbing were her sharp memories of his body pressed against hers in the cab and when they had been entangled on the ground. Despite the bitter weather and her thick clothing, she'd been conscious of his warmth and his body against hers. Was it because she'd not let a man so close in such a long time? What was this odd reaction she was having to a stranger? Whatever it was she had to put a stop to it. Nothing about it was healthy.

Rick had done a good job of driving but the going had been slow. The snow had slackened but the bitter wind had picked up. When Rick stopped at the emergency department door Lauren hurried inside to let the staff know they had arrived. Earlier Rick had radioed ahead, telling the hospital they were on their way.

She headed straight for the unit desk, which was draped with garlands and red and gold Christmas balls. The clerk, wearing reindeer antlers, looked up.

"Hey, I'm Lauren Wilson from Last Stop. I've got two patients in the car. One needs a wheelchair."

Lauren didn't wait for her response before returning to her patients.

Paxton, as she suspected, had climbed out of the car in order to assist their patient.

She rushed to him. "I'll take care of Mr. Thompson. You should be concerned about your hands."

"He's my responsibility," Paxton growled through pain she was sure he was trying to hide.

"And you're mine," she snapped.

Glancing behind her, Lauren was pleased to see the unit staff hurrying toward them with a wheelchair.

She pointed to Mr. Thompson. "He needs the chair."

Mr. Thompson settled into his chair and Paxton walked into the hospital beside him. She and Rick followed close behind them. When Paxton reached the unit desk he said, "I'm Dr. Paxton Samuels. I need to speak to the attending."

Lauren hurried forward. "I'll take care of giving report. You're a patient as of now and you need to worry about having those hands properly tended."

"They're fine."

"Doctors never make good patients," she muttered.

"I heard that," Paxton said with a glare. "I'm sure my fingers have recovered."

"I think we need to get a second opinion. Last Stop needs a doctor with good hands."

He gave her a stricken look then nodded. "Okay, but I want to be informed about my patients."

"Not a problem."

"Hey, Lauren," Henry, a doctor and friend who was wearing a Santa hat on his head, said as he came up the hall toward them.

"Hi, Henry." She gave him a smile.

"What do you have for us tonight?" Henry looked at Paxton with curiosity.

"You've already gotten one of our accident victims, Lewis Williams. Head trauma and hypothermia. We have another head trauma, Art Thompson—" she pointed toward a cubicle where he'd been taken "—in there who needs to be seen."

"I'm Doc—" Paxton tried to butt in.

Lauren didn't slow down. She gestured to Paxton. "This is Dr. Samuels. He's a possible frostbite case."

Henry told a nurse who had just joined them, "Take him to trauma three and get him started on the frostbite protocol. I'll see the head trauma you brought in first. Lauren, come with me and tell me what's going on."

Throughout the brief exchange Paxton looked from her to Henry and back again. He appeared puzzled by their discussion. A couple more times he made noises as if he was going to interrupt but before he could utter anything the unit tech pushed him away.

Lauren stowed her outer clothing behind the nurses' station and joined Henry in Mr. Thompson's room. He was sitting up and talking to the nurse. Lauren shared what she knew about his case. A few minutes later they were on their way to Paxton's room.

"So, who is this Dr. Samuels?" Henry asked.

"Our new temp doctor until we can find someone to permanently replace Dr. Barden. Dr. Samuels was on his way to Last Stop and came up on the accident. He wasn't well dressed for the occasion. I can't complain about his care and quick action, though."

She and Henry stepped into Paxton's cubicle. He was sitting in a chair with his hands in water.

"How's Lewis doing?" he asked before either of them could say anything.

"He's in a room," Henry stated. "He still hasn't regained consciousness. We scanned for swelling but saw nothing. It's just a waiting game now."

"And Mr. Thompson?"

"He seems to be recovering. He has a handful of stitches and we're going to keep him overnight for observation." Henry stepped closer to Paxton. "Now it's your turn. I'm Dr. Henry Fields and I understand you're a doctor as well."

"Dr. Paxton Samuels."

"I hear you're going to fill in at Last Stop."

"Yeah, if I ever get there," he said in a grouchy tone.

Henry gave a dry chuckle. "I've heard of the difficulty. So, tell me, how're your fingers? Our winters are pretty brutal here."

"Better."

"Good to hear."

Paxton lifted his hands out of the water and flexed his fingers. He looked directly at her. Lauren's middle fluttered. He had deep green eyes. Green like the plain in the spring. Their new doctor was handsome.

"I had good care on the way here."

Henry glanced at her. "I have no doubt you did. I should admit you, but Mr. Thompson took the last bed. The best I can offer you is a spot in the waiting room. You really should have someone checking on you every couple of hours."

Rick stuck his head into the cubicle. "Lauren, I've been called out. I've got to go. I'll pick you up in the morning or get someone to come get you." He raised a hand and was gone.

He didn't even give her a chance to respond. She and Dr. Samuels were stuck in Lippscomb.

Paxton's unnerving eyes met hers. "Isn't that our ride back to Last Stop?"

She nodded. "Yep. I guess we're staying the night in the waiting room."

"What about that hotel across the street? I saw it as

we pulled in. Surely they have rooms." Paxton was in no mood to sit up all night in a brightly lit public area.

Lauren shrugged. "I guess that'll work. The weather is too bad to ask anyone to come get us."

"He's—" Henry indicated Paxton "—going to need you to check on him a couple of times during the night. I'm concerned he might spike a fever." Henry looked at her then at Paxton. "And you, I want you to promise you'll keep your hands covered for the rest of the winter season. You'll have trouble again if you're not careful."

"Thanks. I'm well acquainted with frostbite, as I'm from Boston. We have the cold and snow as well."

"Then you know it's nothing to mess around with." Henry wasn't letting his patient intimidate him.

Lauren shook her head in disbelief. Could this evening get any more interesting? "Then we're going out in the weather again." She winced. "More fun in the snow."

"It looks like it."

Lauren imagined Paxton's arrival in Oklahoma was far above and beyond his Bostonian expectations.

"How soon can I get out of here?" Paxton asked Henry.

"As soon as you're ready." Henry made a note on the chart he held. "After you have your hands wrapped. They need to be that way for at least twenty-four hours. I don't want you using them until tomorrow. I'm going to prescribe you a little something for pain. Call me with any problems."

Paxton didn't look pleased with that directive but he didn't argue. "Understood."

Henry nodded to her and Paxton, then left. A few

minutes later a nurse wrapped Paxton's fingers indi-
vidually in gauze.

As soon as she left Paxton said, "I'm ready to go."
He stood and started pulling on his coat.

Lauren assisted him with getting his arms into it,
then adjusted the weight around his shoulders and
buttoned it. The rigid posture of Paxton's body let
her know he wasn't used to people doing things for
him and he didn't like feeling incapable. She pulled
his collar up around his neck.

A funny feeling came over her and she looked up
to see him intently watching her. Her gaze met his. A
pang of awareness ran through her.

His hair was still damp and mussed, a large lock
of it having fallen over his forehead, giving him an
endearing disheveled appeal. He was a good-looking
man, not in a glossy magazine manner but in the sub-
tle way of someone who had confidence in who they
were and what they wanted.

"Can we go now?" he asked with arched eyebrows.

Had she been staring at him? She backed away.
"I need to get my coat and bag on the way out. I left
them at the nurses' station." They walked to the unit
desk. There she went around to a cubby and gathered
her things. "Jane," she said to the unit clerk, "do you
know where we can get some scrubs?"

The heavy woman in her mid-twenties said, "Yeah,
but I'm really not supposed to hand those out."

"I'll bring them back, I promise. If I don't, you can
charge me for them."

Jane pursed her lips and gave her a sideways look.
"In this case..." She went into the storage room. She

soon returned with green scrubs sealed in clear plastic. "Sorry, I only have one set left, in extra-large."

"Okay. We'll make them work." Lauren took the package, then turned to Paxton. "You ready for this?"

"I've been ready," he grumbled.

Apparently he'd had all he wanted for a day. She looked at him. His eyes were bloodshot, underlined by the bruise-like evidence of exhaustion, and his mouth was a tight line. She glanced at his hands all wrapped in white. He deserved to be testy.

Pulling on her coat, she zipped it closed and put her bag over her shoulder. The large automatic glass doors opened as they approached. A blast of cold rolled in. Lauren shivered and murmured, "All we have to do now is manage to not slip on the ice."

Paxton grunted and hunched against the wind, putting his hands into his coat pockets.

She picked her way down the curved drive to the street while keeping an eye on him. All he needed was to fall. Thankfully the street lights gave off enough light to make visibility good and the snow had slowed to drifting flakes. The motel was straight across the four-lane street from the hospital. They waited for a car to pass then as quickly as possible walked toward the window with the glowing orange neon sign that read "Office."

"How often do you get snowbound with a patient?" Paxton asked.

"I'd have to say this is a first."

"I'm not surprised. That's my life lately. A lot of firsts."

Lauren wasn't sure what that statement meant but it didn't sound good by the tone of his voice. Keeping a steady pace, they kept moving. The situation was movie-worthy. They would laugh about this one day.

Lippscomb Motel was a nineteen-fifties-style place, where the one-story building formed a horseshoe and the parking was in front of each room. All the slots appeared taken. What were they going to do if there were no rooms? Return to the hospital. She should have thought to call. They had no choice now but to ask.

Making it to the entrance first, she opened the glass door, letting him go in ahead of her. The warmth of the lobby greeted them.

A bald-headed man wearing a T-shirt despite the weather stood behind a counter with a tiny, sad-looking Christmas tree on it. A TV blared in the background.

"Can I help you?"

"We need a couple of rooms for the night," Paxton stated.

"Don't have but one," the man said off-handedly.

Lauren had been afraid of that.

The man continued, "The storm has us all full up tonight."

"We'll take it," Paxton said before she had a chance to say differently.

She pulled her wallet from her bag.

"I've got this." Paxton put a card on the counter.

Regardless of the circumstances, it didn't quite sit right with her to have a man she hardly knew pay for their hotel room for the night. Somehow it seemed sleazy. She was a professional taking care of a patient who happened to be a male, she sternly reminded herself. There was nothing immoral about that. It was necessary.

A minute later the man returned Paxton's card and gave her a plastic keyring with the number three on it. "The heat won't be on, but it shouldn't take long for it to warm up."

She shuddered at the thought of going back out in the frigid night and to a cold room but she had no choice.

Walking under the awning, they made their way to Room Three. Her feet were wet and cold and all she wanted to do was have a hot bath, call Shawn and crawl into bed. She was pretty sure Paxton had a similar desire.

Unlocking the door, Lauren pushed it wide and let him enter, then quickly closed the door behind them. It wasn't much warmer inside than out. She left Paxton in the middle of the room lit only by the porch light coming through the thin curtains. Going to the lamp sitting on the table between two beds, she clicked it on. The room was much as she had expected.

The beds were standard size with headboards fixed to the wall and a small, well-worn sofa set against a wall with a cheaply framed picture above it. There was a built-in desk with a chair and beside it a clothes rack attached to the wall, level with her head, to serve as the closet.

She was confident it was a major step down from what Paxton must be used to. To his credit, his face didn't look as disgusted as she expected. It leaned toward pitiful. He'd had a hard first day on the job. Yet he'd been more than efficiently competent under the circumstances. Too bad his tenure at Last Stop would be brief.

He sank onto the side of the bed closest to the door.

"Let's get some heat going in here." She hurried to the wall heater located under the only window. It made a clang when she turned on the fan and cranked the thermostat up as high as it would go. "Hopefully it won't take too long for it to heat the place."

"That would be nice. I'm starting to fear that I might never be warm again."

"I'll see if there's a heater in the bathroom." Somehow she had assumed personal responsibility for him. He was new to town. She wanted him to appreciate where she lived, to make a good impression. Even though he was only going to stay a short while she didn't want his time there to leave negative memories. Granted, it had been his choice to come to Oklahoma but still she wished it could have been more welcoming than the last few hours had been.

It was a relief to see there was a heater in the bathroom as well. She turned it on high. When she returned to the main part of the room Paxton still sat in the same spot. That could only be an indication of how bad he felt.

He looked at her. "Sorry about the room situation but at least you don't have to get out in the cold to check on me. We're both adults, I believe we can handle one night together in a hotel room. You needn't worry. I'm no threat, especially tonight."

She wasn't as worried about him as she was about making a fool of herself around him. A shiver went up her spine. He was watching her.

"I can handle it if you can. Uh...you hungry? I

could call for some takeout. There's a pizza place next door."

"Yeah. I could do with something to eat."

"Pizza do?"

"Sure. Anything at this point would be great."

She clasped her hands in front of her. "I'm sorry. This wasn't an ideal way to start a new job. Not very hospitable of the weather."

"Can't control that. I've been through difficult times. Let's just say that today was mild compared to some things I've dealt with."

She'd had her share of difficult times as well. Like losing a husband. Being a single mother. Maybe Paxton wasn't as soft as the fine cut of his coat or the brand name of his shoes implied. After the last few hours she suspected that, like his hands, his life had had some rough spots. "I need to make a phone call then I'll go get that pizza. I'll just step in the bathroom to talk."

Paxton wasn't sure exactly when he'd entered this surreal vortex in time and space where his life had gotten completely out of his control, but he had to find a way to take back some degree of it soon. If two weeks ago someone had predicted that he would be in Oklahoma stranded in a motel room with a pretty young woman who turned out to be his office nurse as well as his personal caretaker during a blizzard, he would have called them a quack. He should be on his honeymoon in the Mediterranean. With a cheat.

He listened to the soft burr of Lauren's voice. "Hi, sweetheart. I'm not going to make it home tonight.

I'll see you tomorrow." There was a pause. "I love you too."

So she had a boyfriend. He noted she hadn't told the guy she was spending the night with him in a hotel room. Paxton harrumphed. As if he could do anything about it even if he had a chance. All he could think about was getting a hot bath and climbing into bed. The medicine he'd been given made him want to do nothing but sleep.

When Gabriella had pulled her final dramatic stunt, he'd never believed it would lead to him having potential frostbite and spending the night in a seedy motel with a woman. He and Gabriella had been an off-and-on couple most of their youth. Their families were close, ran in the same social circle of longtime Bostonians with the correct pedigrees. As adults, it seemed that both sets of parents had expected them to marry. Paxton had cared about Gabriella and had believed she'd felt the same about him. His parents had been encouraging him to marry her for years. For once he had been doing something they blessed.

He'd always been a bit of a rebel in their eyes. He'd gone to a West Coast college instead of the Eastern one all the family members had attended. Between college and medical school, he'd secretly applied to the Peace Corps and spent a year helping in a North African medical clinic. His parents had been vocally displeased. They had anticipated he would finish his medical training and join the clinic that held their family name. Many a time he'd seen disapproval on their faces. It wasn't until he and Gabriella had become engaged that he'd finally felt they were proud of him.

Apparently, and most disconcertingly, Gabriella had found him wanting as a potential mate.

Lauren emerged from the bathroom, slipping her cell phone into her pants pocket. She definitely caught his interest with her glorious mass of long dark hair, smooth skin with cheeks still rosy from the cold and those dark eyes that were intelligent while at the same time tender and caring. Even with her heavy coat on, he suspected there were nice curves beneath. Lauren's wholesomeness was appealing after Gabriella's contrived sophistication.

"I'm going to go see about some food now. I'll be back as soon as I can."

Feeling a vulnerability he hated, he had no choice but to ask, "Uh...before you go, could you help me out of these damp clothes?"

Her eyes widened and her full-lipped mouth went slack.

Where had her thoughts gone? He held up his bandaged hands. "I don't think I can unbutton my coat. Or my shirt for that matter."

It rubbed him the wrong way to need her help. How did it look? Here he was the new physician in town who was supposed to take care of others and he couldn't even take care of himself. He wasn't making a good impression, he was sure. If he wasn't careful Lauren would be the one people turned to instead of him.

Her look had changed from one of surprise to sympathy as she looked at his hands. "I'm sorry. I should've thought. Doesn't make me look like much of a nurse."

"I'd disagree with that. I saw you in action today."
He stood.

Lauren appeared small and fragile in front of him
but there was strength there, he knew. Her warmth
seeped into him as she continued into his personal
space. A handful of her hair fell over her face, stir-
ring his awareness further. What did it feel like? Was
it as silky as it looked? He inhaled. She smelled of the
outdoors. Fresh, clean. Alive.

"Well, let's get your coat off, then I'll help you
with your shirt." Her fingers worked the buttons of
his jacket, opening all of them before pushing it off
his shoulders and throwing it on the bed.

She hesitated before her hands moved to his shirt.

Paxton didn't miss the tremor in her hands. "This
isn't your first time to undress a ma...uh, patient?"

"No. I trained in a big hospital." A firmness had
entered her voice. "Cut a number of patients' clothes
off as well."

Was she reminding him this was strictly business
for her? Which it should be. But her hair looked so
silky. That wasn't something he should be thinking.
Even if being strangers was keeping them apart he
still couldn't take a chance on being rejected. His self-
esteem was battered enough. Besides, they were going
to be working together. "I don't think that will be necessary this time."

Her gaze held a twinkle as it met his for a second
before she continued to work the buttons of his shirt.
He couldn't deny his body's reaction to her standing
so close. Whether he knew her or not. He suddenly
felt warm all over. From his vantage point her movements were the efficient and functionary ones of a

nurse except for the tremor of her hands. At least he wasn't the only one affected. "I'm sorry you have to do this. It's embarrassing to be so helpless."

Lauren worked quickly. "Hey, it happens to all of us sometime. It's just your turn this time."

"That doesn't mean I have to like it."

She smiled. It was a nice one. "I'd just put it down to this entire evening being unusual." Her tone turned matter-of-fact.

As she finished he said, "Now I'm reaching for a new level of mortification." Would his male ego survive this? "I hate to say this but I'm going to need help with my pants button as well."

Lauren smiled. "I've heard that it's good for a doctor to be a patient every once in a while. It gives them more empathy for their patients."

"Then I'll have that in abundance." His disgust rang loud and true.

She freed his pants button. "I think you can handle things from here. And I'm hungry. I'm going after that pizza."

He was hungry too, and on the verge of being turned on.

Seconds later a draft of wind brushed over him before the door closed and he was alone. Paxton eyed the bed. He was going to lie down while she was gone. His fingers tingled as if little pins were being pushed into his skin. Maybe if he raised them above his heart they wouldn't hurt so much.

A bath could wait. He finished removing his clothes, leaving them in a pile on the floor. Removing the pants of the scrub set from the package, he pulled them on. Lauren could have the top.

He slipped between the cold sheets that made the skin of his bare back ripple. Piling one pillow on top of the other, he placed them above his head before he pulled the covers into place. He raised his hands and rested them on the pillows. He shivered until sleep took him. The only time he'd been warm in the last two weeks had been when Lauren had stood near him.

Lauren made her way across the parking lot, grateful for the chilling wind after the hot moments she'd spent with who was in essence her new boss, a stranger. Her credibility as a nurse had never been more in question than when she had been undoing Paxton's pants. Thoughts that were better left dormant had been projected in 3D, full-color, jumbo size.

She'd glanced at Paxton to find a wicked gleam in his jade-colored eyes. Heat rushed to her cheeks at the memory. That had been no patient and nurse moment. It had been about two people attracted to each other on the most basic of human levels. She'd hurried through the process with shaking hands. Even as she'd unbuttoned his shirt her blood had hummed with ultra-sensitive awareness. She had left it hanging open, but not before she'd noticed his chest had a light dusting of hair over well-formed muscles. She forced herself to swallow.

It had been too long since she'd been with a man if her overreaction was any indicator. It wasn't like her not to remain professional in that type of situation. It was a relief to get some fresh air, even if it was still snowing. There hadn't been a time in her life she could remember when she'd been so affected by a man. Even undressing her husband hadn't made her hands tremble. She and Paxton hadn't come anywhere near having sex yet her nerves were still humming as if they had. This instant attraction wasn't a feeling she was familiar with.

Lifting her face to the night sky, Lauren let the few flakes of falling snow settle on her hot skin. Paxton wouldn't be the last doctor to fill in. He wasn't going to stay long, and she certainly wasn't going to let history repeat itself. She'd left town with a man before and she didn't plan to do that again. With her next relationship, she would know the man long enough to know she could trust him. She deserved fidelity. Shawn needed a stable life. That she would give him.

Mark had been a brash young man who had come to town with an oil company. He'd led the team planning to take a number of the wells deeper. She'd been swept off her feet.

Before she'd known it, she was married and on her way out of town with him to his next assignment. She'd dreamed of leaving Last Stop all her life and when she'd got the chance she'd been thrilled. She'd happily packed her bags and left with fairy-tale dreams. At first, everything had been great. They'd moved every three to four months and she'd found every new place exciting but increasingly lonely.

More than once she'd feared Mark wasn't being faithful. He'd always assured her that he was but while at a party she had been approached by a woman who'd told her she'd been seeing her husband. Their marriage had gone from bad to worse.

Only because they'd moved again and she'd discovered she was pregnant had she stayed. She'd told Mark the morning of the accident she was pregnant and had wanted him to find a job that would let them settle down, so they could work on their marriage and be a family. They'd fought, him stating he wanted no part in her plans. That afternoon he was gone. An explosion on the oil rig had killed him and five others.

Lauren had returned to the only place she'd ever really known as home—Last Stop. She'd used Mark's life insurance money to finish nursing school and had made a home for Shawn and herself. He was her life now. No guy passing through town was ever going to turn her head again. Especially some fancy doctor from Boston.

Enough of those thoughts. She had food to get. The pizza place only had a lone young man working. She ordered a large pepperoni pizza and sat down to wait. It had been so long since she'd felt anything for a man. Henry had been asking her out for a couple of months and she had been putting him off. Then in had come a man she knew nothing about and bam! She'd babbled and tingled all over. It just wasn't right. Yet there was an excitement between them she couldn't deny.

Half an hour later she returned to the hotel room with a pizza box in hand and two cans of drink in a bag. She knocked lightly on the door, giving Paxton a heads-up that she was entering. Digging the key out of her pocket, she opened the door. She pushed inside, expecting to find him watching TV. Instead the chair was empty and Paxton was softly snoring in the bed. Compassion filled her. He must have been exhausted after driving all day, then the adrenaline rush of the accident followed by the dangerous brush with frostbite.

Lauren placed the food on the desk before taking

the spare blanket off the top of the clothes rack. She spread it over him. He mumbled, shifted and settled again. Picking up the TV remote, she returned to the desk chair with plans to watch a show while she ate. Paxton could have cold pizza. He needed his rest.

She finished her food, then picked up the scrub top he'd left lying on the bed. Placing the back of her hand on Paxton's forehead, she decided he was a little warm but not overly so. After turning the heat down in the room to a more reasonable temperature, she headed to the bathroom.

After the wonderful experience of a hot shower, she pulled on the scrub top, thankful it was extra-large and hung far enough down her legs to decently cover her. The idea of sleeping in her damp clothes or, worse, nude made her shudder. After hanging and draping their clothes around the room to dry, she sat on her bed. She'd decided that leaving the light on in the bathroom would make it easy to check on Paxton.

Lauren turned off the TV then looked at him sleeping in the next bed. He was resting comfortably. He'd turned on his side but his hands were still above his head. She could only think that they must have hurt. She couldn't help but feel sympathy for his plight. He looked miserable with his bandaged hands. Taking a pillow from her bed, she raised his head and tucked it beneath before easing him down onto it. Satisfied she hadn't disturbed his slumber, she adjusted the covers over his shoulders. Switching off the bedside lamp, she got into bed and was soon asleep.

A loud moan startled her awake. She jerked around to look at Paxton. He whimpered again, then kicked the covers back, leaving most of his body exposed.

The scrub pants rode low on his hips. Climbing out of bed, Lauren reached out to touch his head. Heat surrounded him. Her heart thumped. He had a fever.

Grabbing her digital thermometer from her bag, she ran it across his forehead. It read one hundred and three point seven. She'd been afraid this might happen. Hopefully it would be a temporary situation and not require hospitalization. Returning to her bag, she found fever-reducing medicine then went to the bathroom, filled a water glass and returned to Paxton's bedside.

Lauren shook his shoulder. His skin was hot and dry. She bit her bottom lip as anxiety flooded her. This didn't need to turn into more than a fever. "Paxton."

He groaned but didn't open his eyes.

She shook him a little harder. "Paxton."

"Uh...?" His eyes opened. A glassy unseeing look filled with confusion.

"You have a fever." Her voice was firm. "You need some medicine. Will you sit up?"

He attempted to rise but fell back again, too weak to move. Lauren reached behind his back and supported him until he was upright enough to drink safely. Slipping the pills between his rosy, dry and cracked lips, she pushed them past his teeth onto his tongue, then pressed the glass against his slack mouth to encourage him to drink. He took a sip.

"You need to drink all of it. You're dehydrated." She coaxed him to comply by offering him the glass again.

He took two more swallows before he collapsed back against the pillow.

Carefully freeing her hand, Lauren set the glass

down in order to pull the covers up over his torso and straighten them around him. Paxton had fallen back into a fitful sleep. She dampened a washcloth and applied it to his forehead.

His eyelids fluttered open then closed. He moaned and pawed at the washcloth until it slipped off, but Lauren returned it. She pulled the desk chair up next to the bed then went to re-dampen the cloth. The medicine should kick in soon. Sitting, she lifted the covers from his chest enough that she could sponge him off in an effort to lower his temperature.

She looked at him closely. He really was a fine-looking man. A shadow of his beard was beginning to show, giving him a devil-may-care look. There were small laugh lines around his eyes. She liked people who laughed. There wasn't enough of that in her life. She watched her hand move the cloth over his chest, appreciating the ripples of the muscles beneath his skin. He must do some type of workout to keep them that toned. Even his biceps were well defined.

Sometime later, Paxton started to shake with chills. Pulling the blanket off her bed, she placed it over him and tucked it around him. At least his fever had broken. She dampened the washcloth again and continued to sponge him off.

He murmured something Lauren couldn't understand and thrashed around. Then said, "Gabriella, how could you?"

Lauren rested her hand on his shoulder, hoping to get him to relax. "Shh, you're okay. Everything is all right."

He eased back against the pillow.

When he was calm, Lauren checked his temperature. The reading was normal and she returned to bed.

Who was Gabriella? His wife? Girlfriend? What
had she done? Why was he out here without her?

CHAPTER THREE

PAXTON OPENED HIS eyes to the dim light of morning coming through faded curtains. Where was he? Oh, yeah, a hotel room. He looked at his hands, still bandaged. At least he wasn't feeling any pain.

Turning his head, he saw Lauren sprawled out on the bed next to his with one leg out from under the sheet. The scrub shirt had ridden up, leaving an expanse of shapely thigh visible. Beautiful. Was Lauren's skin as smooth as it looked?

He looked away. Ogling a woman while she slept wasn't his style. Especially women he didn't know. She'd been kind to him and deserved better. After what Gabriella had done he should be leery of women. Yet there was something about Lauren.

Seconds later she rolled over and met his gaze. "You're awake. How're you feeling?"

"Like a bus hit me."

She grinned. "I'm not surprised. Your fever was pretty high last night."

"It was?"

"Yeah, but the medicine brought it down."

He raised his hand to his forehead, taking the washcloth off. "What's this?"

"I was trying to make you more comfortable."

He looked at the chair then at her. "Did you sit up with me?"

"For a little while."

Great. Once again she had been taking care of him. Could he seem more pitiful? She had to have been just as tired as him last night, yet she'd been up caring for him. "Thanks. I'm sorry you had to do that."

Lauren shrugged. "Not a problem. You could probably use another dose of medicine now." She made a move to get up, then jerked the sheet over her hips, her look meeting his. Seconds later she wrapped the sheet around her, picked up her clothes off the desk and headed for the bathroom.

He couldn't help but grin. Despite Lauren's appearance of complete control, she could be set off kilter.

Within minutes Lauren emerged from the bathroom, but she didn't look at him. Instead she headed straight for her bag with a glass of water in hand. Bringing it and some pills, she handed them to him. He swung his legs over the side of the bed and sat up unsteadily.

One of her hands instantly came to his shoulder. "Whoa, no quick moves until we know how you feel."

There was that helplessness again. The hits to his self-esteem just kept on coming.

She stood over him while he swallowed the medicine.

"You do know I can do this by myself?"

Lauren removed her hand and took the glass. "I realize that but it would look bad for me to lose our new doctor on my watch."

Paxton missed the warmth of her touch. "You didn't think I would take it?"

"It's my job to see that you do." Returning to the bathroom, she brought back a filled glass. "You need to drink it all. You lost a lot of fluid last night."

He swallowed all the water and placed the glass on the table then started to unwrap the gauze from his fingers.

"What're you doing?" A note of panic entered her voice.

Paxton didn't stop what he was doing. "I want to see what they look like. The feeling seems to have returned."

When he had difficulty with one section, she huffed and sat across from him. "Let me help." She slowly and carefully removed the bandaging.

"You have gentle hands. You must be a good nurse, Lauren."

"I like to think so." Her eyes never left her work. She turned his hands over in hers a couple of times. Using her index finger, she slowly ran it down the center of his palm and out to the end of his finger. "Can you feel that?"

"I can." It was a tingle that had nothing to do with frostbite. He removed his hand from hers and looked at it himself. "I think they'll heal well."

"Let me have the other one." She reached for his wrapped hand.

Paxton watched the top of her head as she leaned over his hand. Her hair was so dark that it shone like hot cocoa in the light. This time he couldn't resist touching it. Taking a strand between his fingers, he let it skim between them.

Her gaze met his in question.

"I'm sorry. I just couldn't resist." He pulled his hand away and finished unwrapping the gauze. What was his problem? He was going to scare her. She would think he was some needy pervert who was after her. That was the furthest thing from reality. A relationship of any type wasn't on his agenda. He'd been burnt and he had no plans to go back for more. "I wanted to see if I had all the feeling back in my hands."

Her look lingered on him, making him feel self-conscious enough that he stood and walked toward the bathroom.

"I'm hoping that fever last night was only from acute trauma and not infection. You need to take fever-reducing medication regularly for the next few days just to make sure." Lauren stood as well.

"Thanks, Doc," he quipped.

She said to his back, "It has been my experience that doctors make the worst patients."

"I might resemble that." He closed the bathroom door between them.

"I'll be right out here if you need me," she called, irritation clear in her voice.

It didn't take him long to shower. Despite his efforts not to admit his discomfort, he had to. Still having an ache in his hands was aggravating. Opening the door a crack, he called, "Hey, can you hand me my clothes?"

"Just a sec." Then he heard her say, "Hey, honey, I have to go. Yes, bye."

She'd been on the phone. Had it been with the same guy? A woman as pleasant and attractive as Lauren surely had someone. Why should that matter to him anyway?

The sound of her moving around then coming back toward him had him waiting. A hand holding his pants and shirt came through the open space.

"Here you go."

"Thanks." He took them from her.

"I called Rick. He'll be here in under two hours. That'll give us time to eat and check on Lewis and Mr. Thompson."

"I'll be ready in a minute." With his pants on and his shirt unbuttoned, he stepped out of the bathroom.

Lauren's lips were pulled in a tight line as she watched him. "You're hurting, aren't you?"

He nodded. "Yeah. I hate to admit it but my fingers don't move well enough to dress myself. And I'm hungry."

"I bet you are. You missed the pizza last night." She stepped to him and matter-of-factly started buttoning his shirt. Having no choice, he accepted it. Done with that, she fastened his pants as if it was no big deal then announced, "We need to get your hands wrapped again."

Soon she was helping him into his coat and pulling hers on, all without any emotion or physical reaction. No shaking of hands or quick breathing. Now his mortification was complete. She could dress him and feel nothing, while desire tugged at his body.

Outside the snow had ended, the air was chilly and the sky blue as they walked across the parking lot.

"I think it would be easiest to go to the hospital cafeteria for breakfast," Lauren suggested. They headed toward the hospital and a few minutes later they walked through the automatic doors, past the welcome desk and into the cafeteria.

"You shouldn't hold a tray. I'll get your food. Just have a seat. What would you like?"

She was right. Could this get more humiliating? When he got the bandages off... He gave his order without hesitation. "Scrambled eggs, bacon and toast. A large cup of coffee."

Lauren nodded and he watched her walk away. They had known each other less than twenty-four hours but he felt like he knew her better than he ever had Gabriella. Lauren was smart, efficient and capable, could take charge yet followed orders when needed. She didn't complain, which heaven knew wasn't one of Gabriella's virtues. Men were attracted to Lauren judging by the way Henry had greeted her and whoever the guy on the phone had been. Paxton certainly felt a fascination.

His own phone rang. With effort, he removed it from his coat pocket. Looking at the caller ID, he saw it was his mother.

"Hello, Mom."

"Paxton, where are you?"

"You know good and well where I am. I'm in Oklahoma."

"Did you really take that job?"

"I told you I was going to. I've already started." He wouldn't tell her it had been on the side of the road in a snowstorm.

"Pax, I can't believe you're doing this to your father. He needs you here."

"We've been through this before. There are plenty of doctors in Boston."

"But your father needs you. You know he's ill."

"Yes, but the treatment is working." His father had been diagnosed with a heart condition.

"He needs you. I need you." She paused for a second then said, "Gabriella called to say she was sorry." His mother's voice was soft.

"Mom, I'm not going to talk about that. It's done." Lauren was on her way back. "I've got to go. I've made a commitment for a month here and I need to honor it. I'll talk to you soon."

"But, Paxton—"

"Got to go, Mom." He hung up just as Lauren reached the table.

"Here you are." She placed a tray with two plates of food on it in front of him. It smelled wonderful. Her gaze fell on the phone but she didn't ask any questions.

"I didn't think to send money with you. And you bought pizza last night. What do I owe you?"

"Don't worry about it. We'll settle up later." Lauren sat across from him.

"Then maybe I can make it up by taking you to dinner one night."

She took one of the plates off the tray and set it on the table across from him. "We'll see."

Lauren had said nothing about not being able to because of a husband or boyfriend. Despite his hands and uncomfortable method of eating he dug into his meal. He took a sip of his coffee. "So, what do I need to know about Last Stop?"

She studied him a moment. "Well, there isn't much to tell. It's part of the panhandle of Oklahoma."

"Panhandle?"

Using her hand, she made a gesture of holding

something. "You know when land boundaries have a strip of land that sticks out like a handle. Look at the shape of Oklahoma on a map sometime. It looks like a frying pan."

Paxton nodded. "I get it."

"There're about a thousand people living in or around Last Stop. Most are farming families or work for the oil industry. But there aren't as many of them as there once were."

"So how long have you lived in Last Stop?" He finished off his eggs.

"All my life."

He could understand that. He'd lived in Boston most of his. Except for his college years and the year in the Peace Corps. "Never left?"

"Only for a short while."

"Why'd you come back?"

A shadow of pain filled her eyes. "Because my husband died and it's home." She put her fork down on a partially eaten plate of food. "I'm going to return the scrubs to ER then check on Lewis and Mr. Thompson. Do you want to wait for me here?"

She'd been married. Her husband had died young. She'd experienced some major trauma. "I'm sorry about your husband. I didn't mean to bring up sad memories. I'm going with you to see Lewis and Mr. Thompson. They're my patients now too." If it hadn't been her husband she'd been speaking to last night, then who had it been?

The moment seemed forgotten and she nodded as if pleased with his statement about their patients. "Then we need to get going. I don't want Rick to have to wait for us. He's taking time out to come get us."

Lewis's parents were with him when they got to his room. He was now awake and seemed okay but was going to have to stay in the hospital one more night.

"I want you in my office next Monday just for a checkup, okay?" Paxton said before leaving the room.

"He'll be there," Lewis's mother promised. "We heard what you did, Dr. Samuels. We appreciate it."

"You're welcome." He'd been thanked before for care he'd given but somehow Lewis's mother's sincerity touched him more than usual.

They moved a few doors down the hall to Mr. Thompson's room. The older man was dressed and waiting for his wife to pick him up.

He stretched out his hand and quickly brought it back to his side. "Sorry, Doc. I forgot about your hands. Thanks for helping last night."

"Not a problem. They'll be better soon. Call me if you start feeling bad for any reason."

Less than an hour after their breakfast they were waiting next to a large Christmas tree in the emergency department for Rick. They didn't have to sit long. Lauren insisted Paxton take the front seat.

"Hey, Rick, I'm ready to go home." She sounded tired. Paxton spent the next hour peppering Rick with questions about Last Stop and the area. When Lauren didn't comment, he glanced back to see that she was asleep. Her night had been as exhausting as his.

His attention returned to the world outside the windshield. It was white with snow. There wasn't even a significant rise or dip in the land for as far as he could see. In his part of the world it snowed but there were buildings and roads, even mountains if he went far enough out of town. Here there was nothing but the road and fence line.

Finally, on the horizon, he could make out a cluster of buildings large enough to make up a town. He watched in anticipation as they approached. No structure was over one story high. His apartment in Boston was on the twelfth floor. Here, the stores were built of wood or cinder block. There was only one intersection, but it had no street light. A few cars were parked on the street. There were Christmas wreaths hanging from each lamppost.

"Well, I see Roger got an early start with the Christmas decorations this morning." Lauren's voice had a rough sound from sleep. It added a charming dimension to her Western drawl.

"Yeah, he was upset that the storm made him wait until today," Rick said. "You want me to drop you off at your place or with the doc here?"

She sat up in the seat. "My car's at the office. I'll just go there."

"I understand that I'm to live in an apartment attached to the office." Paxton looked back over the seat.

"It's a house. The office, a waiting room and exam room are up front. The kitchen and a bedroom and sitting room are in the back. This is it right up here." Lauren pointed ahead of them.

Rick turned right and then took a small street to the left before pulling into a drive on the left beside a clapboard house painted white. There was a sign in the yard that read "Last Stop Clinic." He stopped behind Paxton's car, which was sitting under an open shed.

A large green truck with a double cab that dwarfed his car sat beside it but not under the cover.

Paxton had needed a change in his life and he'd certainly gotten it.

Lauren watched as Paxton took in his home for the next few weeks. He looked both amazed and dazed. What had he expected? She'd woken to find Rick busy telling Paxton about the area around Last Stop. She liked the sound of Paxton's voice. Deep, soothing with an occasional clip on the end of words. That was a place she didn't need to go. She'd already been swept off her feet by a man who had come to town for a short stay. Being whisked off again wasn't in her plans.

"Thanks, Rick, for the ride. Also, thanks for having my car brought in." Paxton climbed out of the car.

"No problem. See you later," Rick called.

Lauren was grateful someone had shoveled the snow off the walk. If Paxton fell, he might be forced to hightail it back to Boston. Opening the door of the clinic, she turned on some lights.

"I'll give you a quick tour before I go home and change." She turned around in the open space. "This is the waiting room." A few chairs and a table were set against one wall, on the other a desk. She stepped to a door off the main room. "This is your office."

It was a simple room with a large oak desk in the center that she'd loved to play around as a child when she'd visited Dr. Barden. With Paxton's background, would he be as impressed with it? He was probably used to glass and chrome. She led the way down the hall. "This room—" she stopped at an open door "— is an exam room." She stepped farther down the hall.

"Here is another. On down here is your living area."
She moved into what was a small kitchen.

"What's all this?" Paxton's voice rose in exasperation.

Taking up every spot on his kitchen counter and
small table were bags of food, casserole dishes and
cakes.

Lauren giggled. "You've been visited by the welcome wagon."

"The what?" His brows rose.

"Some of the women just brought you some food
to say welcome and thank you. I'm sure they all heard
about what you did last night."

"But all this!" He waved his hand around in disbelief.

"Everyone in Last Stop knows you're in town."

He groaned. "I have more food than I can eat."

She grinned. "Far more. Even my mom has a casserole in here somewhere."

Paxton looked perplexed, as if it had never occurred to him that the town would be glad to see
him. "Haven't you ever had someone welcome you
with food?"

He was looking through the food, reading the la-
bels. "Never."

"You'll find things might be a little different around
here." Lauren stepped toward another open door.

Paxton followed her. "I'm starting to learn that in
more ways than one."

"This is your bedroom and a sitting area where
there is a TV."

She had to admit it wasn't much, but he would be

comfortable enough for the amount of time he would be staying.

"The bathroom is through there." She walked in front of him to point out a small door inside the room. "I see someone brought in your suitcase and belongings."

There was a skeptical note in his voice when he asked, "Did Dr. Barden live here?"

"No, it's mostly been used when there has been a late night or maybe a patient needed to be watched closely until the ambulance got here. That type of thing. It's been cleaned and readied for you, though. Sorry there was no other place for you to stay."

"This'll be fine." He didn't sound disappointed. Her face brightened. She'd feared he might be upset with the accommodations.

"Is there anything you need before I go? If not, I'm headed home for a change of clothes and will be back in an hour. Thankfully this was our morning off, but we have afternoon clinic today if you're up to it."

"I'm up to it." Paxton caught her hand as she went by him, stopping her. "I want to thank you. You were great last night at the accident and then taking care of me. Maybe I should be giving you some food."

She smiled, trying to cover her reaction to his touch. A tingle ran through her. She'd known Paxton less than twenty-four hours and she shouldn't be having this reaction. They had to work together. He wasn't staying around long. She tugged on her hand. He released it. "That's not necessary. Just be careful with those hands while I'm gone."

"I will." He raised a wrapped hand. "Promise."

She felt guilty leaving him there looking rather

abandoned but she needed some space along with a new set of clothes, and most of all, she wanted to give her son a hug. "I've got to go. Someone's expecting me."

CHAPTER FOUR

WHO WAS SHE rushing off to see? Paxton would find out when she came in later.

What had possessed him to take her hand? They had been thrown together for one night. He shouldn't be reacting to Lauren on such a primitive level. For heaven's sake, he'd just come out of a horrible situation. Being attracted to another woman so soon shouldn't be happening. He couldn't even trust his own judgment. He'd certainly been wrong where Gabriella was concerned.

He'd believed his and Gabriella's affections had gone deep enough that he had asked Gabriella to marry him. Then had her cheat on him and his parents think he should forgive her and marry her anyway. All to save the family name. Was his ego so bruised he'd go after the first woman he found attractive? Lauren deserved more consideration than that. He wanted to believe *he* was better than that. Yet his physical reaction to her was undeniably strong.

He looked around the room as the sound of her footsteps disappeared down the hall. He should get his act together. First thing he had to do was put on a clean change of clothes, warmer ones. After that he would familiarize himself with the clinic.

It was a struggle, but he managed to remove his clothes and put fresh ones on. Memories of Lauren helping him dress and undress flitted through his mind. Their relationship had had a unique beginning.

Relationship?

They had no bond outside her being his nurse for the next four weeks. It would remain that way. Despite his unusual attraction to her they were just co-workers. And for all he knew, this "someone" she kept talking to and about was her boyfriend. He certainly wasn't going to encroach on someone else's woman.

Going to the kitchen, he looked at all the food. When and how was he ever going to eat it all? Still, it was nice to know he was welcome. Finding a plate of cookies, he took a few and headed to the office. It was time to have a look at the "clinic" that would be his workspace for the next few weeks.

It was nothing like what he was used to. There was no stainless steel or glass. Instead, most of the furniture was worn and as if they were leftover pieces. He made his way to the exam room. It appeared adequately stocked. There was a wooden cabinet with a small sink, and shelves above full of supplies. An exam table was located on the wall opposite. He had never seen one except in pictures. It was old but looked sturdy.

Crossing the waiting room, he entered the office. A large oak desk with a high-backed leather chair commanded most of the space. Two comfortable-looking wingback fabric-covered chairs in navy blue were stationed in front of it and behind was a bookcase filled with books and specimen jars. In the back corner was a metal filing cabinet. As he'd guessed, it was filled with patient charts. Paxton grinned. He was used to a handheld electronic tablet and paperless recordkeeping. This job meant stepping back into a simpler time. He had no real idea of what type of problems he would be confronted with but he would find out this afternoon.

The sound of the bell on the front door ringing brought him to the office door. A tall, thin man with a weather-worn face and piercing blue eyes gave Paxton a swift once-over. He held a thick-looking leather hat, wore a heavy coat, jeans and boots. He demanded in a gruff manner, "You the new doctor?"

"Yes, I'm Dr. Samuels."

He turned the hat in his hands as if nervous. "Can I talk to you?"

"Uh…would you mind waiting for a few minutes? Lauren will be here then. I don't quite know where everything is located yet." Once again he was inadequate for the job. Would he be leaning on her the entire time he was here?

An embarrassed look came over the man's face and he glanced toward the door as if considering leaving. "I'd rather this be between you and me."

Curious now, Paxton pointed toward the hall. He could at least listen. "Well, why don't we go to the exam room?"

The man walked down the hallway and Paxton followed. When they were both in the room, the man said, "I heard about the trouble last night. I appreciate you helping Lewis."

"You know Lewis?" News traveled fast around

here. He suppressed a shudder. If any citizen of Last Stop learned of his humiliation in Boston, everyone would know within twenty-four hours.

"I do. People around here talk, but Lewis is also my grandson."

Paxton nodded in acknowledgment. "I see, Mr...?"

"Gerhart."

"Well, Mr. Gerhart, how can I help you?"

"I've been having trouble with, you know, my privates. Burns to pee."

Paxton nodded. Now he understood the need for secrecy. Especially since news traveled so fast in town. "Well, the first thing we should do is get a urine sample. You'll need to fill one of these." Paxton took a plastic cup with a blue top off the shelf, thankful he didn't have to go hunting for one. "There's a bathroom just next door."

The older gentleman accepted the cup with a sheepish look and left the room. He soon returned with the sealed cup in hand and wearing a pained expression. Placing it on the counter, he looked expectantly at Paxton.

He suspected Mr. Gerhart had a urinary tract infection but wouldn't know until the test results were in. "I don't know what the lab situation is yet but I'll see that it's taken care of. I'll give you a call tomorrow in case I need to see you again or call in a prescription." As soon as Lauren returned he would have her see about getting the sample to the lab.

"Thanks, Doc." The man extended his hand. "I appreciate you keeping this between us."

"I'll do the best I can." Paxton shook Mr. Gerhart's hand. "I'll be in touch."

The man nodded, placed his hat on his head and left.

Mr. Gerhart couldn't have been driving down the street long before the bell on the door rang again. This time it was a young woman.

"Can I help you? I'm Dr. Samuels. You are…?"

"I'm Margie Michaels." She raised her hand, which was wrapped in a cloth. "I'm one of the cooks over at the café. I burnt my hand."

"Come to the exam room and let me have a look."

He joined her at the exam table. "I need you to unwrap it and I'll have a look." His own bandages were going to have to go. He needed to do his job. The red angry skin on Margie's hand made him wince. "We'll need to clean it with soap and water. Then wrap it and keep it clean and dry."

"Dr. Samuels, how can I help?" Lauren stepped into the room like a warm breeze. "Hi, Margie. What happened?"

Paxton was relieved to see her. Lauren would be more efficient than he. She knew where things were, knew the patients. Could actually use her hands properly. Nothing about her appearance said typical nurse, yet he was very aware she was an exceptional one.

Her hair was pulled back from her face. She wore a coral sweater that enhanced the natural color of her cheeks and a pair of jeans that hugged her curves in a most complimentary manner. What he really gave his consideration were the Western boots on her feet with their pointed toes.

They weren't the type of footwear he was used to seeing his clinic nurses wearing, in or out of scrubs. The women in his life tended toward three-inch heels and brand names. He redirected his thoughts. "Lauren, we need saline, gauze and a pan."

A minute later she had all the supplies and was busy taking care of the burn. When Lauren finished wrapping the hand, he told Margie, "Come back in a few days and let me have a look again. Take over-the-counter pain medicine as needed."

As soon as Margie left, Paxton removed his bandages. It was time he was a doctor instead of a patient.

Lauren came back into the exam room. "You need to keep those on a little longer."

"Not going to happen. I can't do my job."

She pursed her lips but didn't say anything more. Instead, she ushered in a mother with two small children. He put on his most reassuring smile. "Hi, I'm Dr. Samuels. What seems to be wrong today?"

"They have sore throats," the haggard-looking mother answered.

He deepened his smile as he coaxed the little girl, who was half cowering behind her bigger brother. "Let me have a look and I'll see if I can make you feel better."

The rest of the afternoon went much the same. As the sun was going down he was glad to see the waiting room was finally empty. His hands were hurting, which he had no intention of admitting to Lauren. She'd reminded him a number of times throughout the afternoon that he should be conscious of his hands.

"Well, that was interesting," he said now that it was just the two of them.

"How's that?" Lauren gave him a narrow-eyed look as if she thought he was saying something negative.

"Just that I've not seen those types of problems since I was in the Peace Corps."

"Really?" Surprise lit her voice. "You were in the Peace Corps?"

"Yeah, I spent a year working in clinics all around Africa. Sobering times." And freeing. A year that had him away from his parents and their expectations. He had been his own man. Here in Last Stop he was once again.

"That must have been interesting."

"It was. I was doing good work with people who needed a lot of help."

"As you can see, we need your help here as well." Lauren went about straightening up the waiting room. "You offered good care this afternoon. Even with hurt hands."

"Thanks." It was nice to hear her praise. "Is every day like today?"

"No, sometimes we're busier. Or super-slow. Some of these people drive over an hour to get to a doctor. Dr. Barden moved to the coast four days ago so some of them have been waiting to see you for a while. You can guarantee they're sick when they make that effort."

"That reminds me. I saw a man before you got here."

She turned to look at him. "Who?"

"I'd rather not say. He wanted the visit to remain between us."

"Okay." She sounded curious and maybe hurt as well.

"Anyway, I have a urine sample that needs to be

run. Can you add that to the others going to the lab? By the way, how's all that handled?"

"It has to be sent to Lippscomb. They'll be picked up by a courier in a few minutes. You should have the results first thing in the morning. What name do I need to put on the sample?"

"Don't worry about it. I'll take care of it." He would process the sample and put it in the cooler before the courier came.

"By the way, is there a room or closet not used in the house that I could set up as a small lab? We need to be offering quicker results than the next day, when-ever we can."

She looked back at him. "There's one off the kitchen that's used for storage but doesn't have much in it."

"May I look at it?"

"Sure. I have a few more minutes before I have to go."

He followed her down the hall. "By the way, who do I thank for seeing to it my bed was made?"

She said over her shoulder, "That would be my mom. I called ahead and she came over and put things to rights. I knew you wouldn't feel like it."

"Please tell her thank you for me."

"Will do." She led him to a small door off the kitchen and opened it.

"Why didn't Dr. Barden have a lab?"

"He didn't think it was necessary. He was happy enough with the way things were handled. You'll learn that things change slowly around here." She sounded both resigned and ambivalent. "He was a good doctor to us for forty years." This time her tone rang clearly—tread lightly.

Paxton peered into the open doorway. There were shelves on each side, creating a narrow path to a wooden workbench in the back. Stepping inside, he searched for the light switch. "Is there any light in here?"

Lauren came to stand beside him and reached beneath a shelf. Light flooded the room.

"Had that hidden, didn't you?" Paxton smiled at her.

She grinned and shrugged.

He continued on to the bench. It looked sturdy and was the right height. This space would work quite nicely.

Lauren touched one of the shelves. "Do you think we'd need all these? There would be more room if we took one side out."

"That's a good plan. We'll need a dedicated electric line to support the centrifuge and other equipment. It won't be a fully fledged lab but it'll at least give us some basic answers faster." He moved to the back of the closet and searched for outlets.

Lauren joined him. "I know a couple of people I think would do the work for cost. I'll get in contact with them tomorrow. What about the equipment?"

"I'll handle that." He'd have what they needed shipped out from Boston as soon as possible.

Lauren turned to leave at the same time he did. Paxton bumped into her and she teetered to one side. He grabbed her forearms, keeping her on her feet. Her palms landed on his chest, feeling as if they were branding him. With wide-eyed uncertainty, she stared at him. His gaze dropped to her slightly parted full lips.

What would she do if he kissed her? Could he stop himself?

She pulled her upper lip between her teeth.

"Lauren?"

A woman's voice calling her name barely registered through the haze of anticipated pleasure racing through him.

Lauren abruptly pushed against his chest. Paxton reluctantly straightened and backed away. He took a stabilizing deep breath.

She hurried out of the closet. "Mom, I'm right here," she answered a shade too quickly, sounding breathless. And had there been a slight quaver in her voice as well?

"What're you doing in there?" Her mother stepped to the door.

"We were discussing making the area into a lab." Lauren sounded more in control.

Paxton waited a few seconds before following her out. An older version of Lauren with short hair stood in the middle of the kitchen, watching him.

Lauren's hand shook slightly as she extended it. "Mom, I'd like you to meet Dr. Paxton Samuels. My mom, Sarah Tucker."

Mrs. Tucker smiled. "Hi! It's nice to meet you. I understand you were the hero of the hour last night."

He shrugged. At this rate he might start believing the gossips. "I wouldn't quite put it that way. Your daughter was a great help. I'd take her aid in an emergency any day. It's a pleasure to meet you. And thanks for making my bed and seeing the place was ready for me."

Mrs. Tucker gave him a warm smile. "You're very welcome. I'm just sorry you had such a hard start here in Last Stop."

"Mom brought you soup for dinner. It's on the stove, warming." Lauren didn't look him in the eyes.

"Thank you." His gaze went from daughter to mother. "You've already done too much."

More food. Just what he needed.

"We're just glad you're here. I'd better go now. I know you could use a full night's rest." Lauren's mother smiled and headed back down the hall.

Lauren turned to follow her. "See you in the morning."

Paxton watched her go, regretting the interruption and yet relieved at the same time. He hated he'd missed out on that kiss but it hadn't been a good idea.

No matter how attractive he found Lauren, starting a fling with his nurse showed poor judgment.

Lauren wasn't sure a night spent in her own bed had left her any more refreshed than she had been after her stay in the hotel. Paxton affected her, stirred her passion in more ways than one.

She couldn't fault the way he interacted with the patients. He listened. Took time to hear their complaints. Had been welcoming with the kids. There was nothing of the hurry-up-you-are-a-number mentality she'd anticipated from a big East Coast doctor.

The fact he'd worked in the Peace Corps revealed a side of him she hadn't expect either. Nothing in his online pedigree had adequately prepared her for the flesh-and-blood Paxton who'd been right in there with her, providing emergency medical care for Lewis. Last Stop could have done worse in a replacement doctor.

His official biography had provided all the pertinent information. Paxton was more than qualified for the job. Along with that she had noticed that his last name was the same as the clinic he was associated with in Boston. She couldn't help but be impressed. On another suggested link on the search page she had read something about the wedding of the year having been called off and Paxton's name had been included.

What had happened? Had Paxton been left at the altar? Or maybe he had been the one doing the leaving. She'd been interrupted by Shawn and had never returned to read more. Now her curiosity was piqued.

To make it worse, she found him extremely attractive with his dark good looks. And that almost-kiss... She'd not been prepared for it and yet she would have welcomed it. The bump had been innocent, she was sure.

However, it wasn't like her to kiss someone she didn't know well. A man possibly on the rebound. And there was her young son to consider. She wasn't going to bring someone into Shawn's life who would leave soon. Living in a tiny town meant her reputation was important. She'd been careful to have a good one since returning home and needed to continue doing so, for Shawn's sake.

When her husband had come to town she'd been looking for excitement, something more than had been available in Last Stop. He had offered it. There had been youthful lust and then love between them, but none of the raw sexuality she felt around Paxton. Why was she so very aware of him on that primal level? The one thing she was sure of was that her home was in Last Stop now and Paxton was merely passing through. She had no intentions of repeating the past.

That realization helped her fight the zip of anticipation rushing through her each time she contemplated seeing Paxton again. It had been so long since she'd felt that kind of male/female attraction that a sliver of fear accompanied it. Paxton was essentially her boss for the next month. Then he'd be gone. And they were from two entirely different worlds. He wasn't a man to hang her future on, and yet...he made her feel alive again. No one should know how she was feeling. Especially Paxton. What would it hurt for her to enjoy it while it lasted?

After dropping Shawn off with her mother, Lauren drove to the clinic. She entered the front door and started down the hall.

"Good morning, Lauren."

She looked into the office. Paxton sat behind the desk, studying a laptop screen.

"You're up and at it early this morning," she commented, grateful he was acting as if nothing had happened between them the evening before. For him it probably hadn't been a big deal.

"I could say the same about you. I wanted to check the lab work. My patient will need to come in and have an exam after all."

Lauren harrumphed. "Your mystery patient?"

"Yes, that's the one. But I don't know how to get in touch with him. All I have is his name."

She waited expectantly.

He regarded her with speculative eyes before conceding, "I guess I don't have any choice but to tell you. It's Mr. Gerhart."

"What? He came in. I can't believe it. I've never seen or heard of him going to a doctor."

Paxton looked back at the laptop. "It was him. Lewis's grandfather."

"That's him." She was shocked he'd come the first time and couldn't imagine him doing it a second. "Good luck getting him back in here."

"Then we'll go see him."

She was stunned by his directness. "Okay. But before we do that I'd like to have a look at your hands."

"They're a lot better." His attention returned to the computer screen.

"I'd still like to have a look." She used her firm tone that made Shawn pay attention.

His glance conveyed irritation. "You don't trust my professional opinion?"

"Not when it concerns your personal recovery. Something about you makes me think you don't give your own healthcare anywhere near the attention you give your patients."

Paxton pursed his lips but there was a slight upturn at the corners. "You think you know me that well after less than forty-eight hours?"

"Some things you can discern about a person pretty quickly." Like the idea he might be a great kisser? Those thoughts she'd best keep to a minimum for her sanity's sake.

Paxton's eyes narrowed. "I'm not sure I like being that transparent."

She shrugged, careful to conceal her triumph. "I

still want to have a look at your hands. You want me to do it here or in the exam room?"

"I'm good with here, if you are."

Lauren pulled the chair in front of the desk around to his side. "I see you reapplied bandages. Smart move."

"Okay, so they hurt a little when exposed to cold air. I needed sleep last night."

"We both did. Let me see the right one first." She held out a hand.

Paxton did as she requested. She unwrapped the gauze. His fingers were pink. "Wiggle them for me." Paxton did so. "I'd say you're right. You're on the mend. Let me check the other one."

He huffed but presented his hand. A few minutes later she sat back. "It looks like you will recover with no ill effects but you're going to need to take care of them. Keep them covered outside. This isn't the running from heated building to heated building that you're used to."

"I have to admit I should have taken the time to cover them, but I packed hurriedly and wasn't sure where to find my gloves. My decision to accept this position was rather last minute."

"Why was that?" Would he tell her about the wedding business without her asking?

"Let's just say that's a subject better left alone. So, tell me about a typical week at Last Stop's clinic. One that doesn't include a tractor accident."

She guessed that was as good as a no. So what was he hiding? Lauren wanted to pursue the mystery but instead she said, "As a general rule, the clinic is open Monday through Friday, with Wednesday afternoon off."

"So that means I'd be able to do some shopping tomorrow?"

"Yeah."

He nodded. "Good. Then I'll get some heavier pants, thick socks and adequate gloves. Is Lippscomb where I need to go?"

"That's what I'd suggest. Well, I'd better get busy. I've got some restocking to do in the exam room before our first patient shows up."

She made it as far as the door before Paxton called after her, "I've been meaning to ask you, who's this person you keep talking to and rushing off to?"

His question froze her. He'd been wondering about her personal life? Did he think she had a boyfriend?

She half turned in order to see his face before she answered. "My son, Shawn."

Only the blink of his eyes made her aware of his astonishment.

"Son," he said, more to himself than her, as if he was mulling over the idea. "That one I hadn't expected." Paxton opened his mouth as if he wanted to say more but the bell ringing signaled a patient had arrived.

Their morning went much as the afternoon before with a regular stream of patients. When they did have a break, Paxton went to his office and she did paperwork at her desk.

At noon, he asked, "How's lunch handled around here?"

She smiled. "We usually eat."

"Funny." He grinned.

"I normally bring my lunch and eat in the kitchen. Dr. Barden always went home. Since the kitchen is now your personal space, I'll just eat at my desk."

"I see no reason we can't share the kitchen table. In fact, you don't have to bring your lunch, I've enough food for a year back here." He strolled toward the kitchen. "Which reminds me, I need to do something with all this food."

"I can help with that," she offered. He did sound overwhelmed.

"I'd be grateful."

She wasn't surprised to find that all of it was still set out on the counter. He wouldn't have felt like it or cared enough last night to put it away. With her knowledge of the ladies in town, she was sure the refrigerator held the food that would spoil. Going to the refrigerator, she looked in.

"Heaven's sakes, there's more." His exasperation rang clear.

She glanced back. Paxton was peering over her shoulder. Their mouths were inches apart. For a moment their gazes met, held. Passion rose in his. There was a hint of a dare there.

It was time for her to get a grip. Lauren was old enough to push temptation away. She intended to move out from between him and the refrigerator but that didn't make the situation better when she straightened. Instead, her body brushed against his. From shoulders to hips she felt his warmth. That awareness from the day before had gone from simmering to boiling.

Paxton stepped away, as if he had suddenly realized what was happening and had thought better of it.

The cool air from the refrigerator wasn't strong enough to overcome the heat generated between them. She gestured vaguely. "I, uh, need to get that food put away. I don't know what you had planned for your lunch but there're a couple of casseroles in here you might want to try. Just put some in the microwave."

"You won't join me?"

She couldn't admit that he'd rattled her nerves and she couldn't eat. Instead, she said, "Yeah, I'll have some." Going to a cabinet, she pulled two plates out. "Why don't you sit down and I'll do this."

He looked genuinely grateful and disturbed at the same time. "Thanks. I'm going to owe you big time when I get my hands back and figure out everything around here."

"No problem. Being someplace new always means a learning curve."

She went back to the refrigerator and pulled out a dish. "This is Mrs. Clara's chicken casserole. It's one of my favorites." She put two large spoonsful of casserole on a plate, placed it in the microwave and started it. While it was heating she began putting food away in the cabinets.

At the ding of the microwave she placed the plate on the table in front of Paxton. She pulled out a nearby drawer, found forks and handed him one.

"Will you tell me about the people who live here?"

"I mentioned before that most of them are either farming families that go back generations or are involved in the natural gas industry. My family happens to be a little bit of both. We farm close to a thousand acres. Some cows and growing wheat and grain for livestock. We also have gas wells." She served up her own plate and started it heating.

"I saw some wells, driving up here. First time I've seen the real thing. Before only in pictures. I was expecting more of the tall iron pyramids."

"That's rigging they use when digging a well. When the well is ready to produce, all that is needed is the pump and meters to read the flow."

"Well, you learn something new every day." Paxton acted genuinely amazed and impressed. "Don't see or get much of that kind of thing in Boston."

She grinned. "I don't imagine you do."

"So I'm guessing the people around here are well-to-do."

Lauren chuckled and removed her plate from the microwave. "These are gas wells, not oil. The income was good during my great-grandparents' days. The money is more supplemental now. Occasionally there's a new well drilled but not so much anymore. For the most part people here live simply."

"I like the people I've met so far."

Lauren joined him at the table. "You seem to have made a positive impression on them as well. My mother thought you were very nice."

Thought he was handsome. Asked if he was single.

All questions Lauren didn't want to respond to. It was time for a change in subject despite her own personal curiosity about Paxton. What had brought him here, what his life had been like in Boston…did he have a girlfriend? "Now you know about me, so what about you?"

"It's pretty simple. This opportunity came up. I wanted to do something different and here I am."

Paxton had no intention of admitting he hadn't been enough for the woman he had been set to marry. His ego wouldn't let him even if he'd wanted to reveal that hard-to-swallow truth to Lauren.

"Does your wife or girlfriend mind you being away for so long?"

"I don't have either."

And I'm not looking.

"Just so you know, I sort of looked you up on the internet."

"Sort of?" He watched her closely, trying to judge what she might know.

Lauren shrugged. "Well, more like read about you."

"And what did you learn?" Panic filled him. Had she seen his personal catastrophe on the internet? Hopefully not.

"I learned you're not the only doctor in your family."

This he would talk about. "Yes, my family profession is medicine, but I didn't become a doctor because of that. I wanted to help people and I was interested in medicine."

Lauren's look made him wonder if she saw through that statement, and sensed the unrelenting pressure he would have been under had he refused to become a doctor.

"So how many of you are doctors?" Lauren loaded a fork with food.

"My father and his brother, a couple of cousins and their children are involved in medicine in some way."

Her look turned thoughtful. "Apple didn't fall far from the tree."

"I guess not." Paxton wasn't sure if that was a compliment or not. He hoped he was different in some very fundamental ways. He'd tried hard enough, and was still trying. That was enough about him.

"Have you always lived in Boston?"

"I'm like you, I left for a little while but have always returned." He couldn't hide out here forever this time either. He would return to Boston. There really wasn't a choice now his father's heart disease was progressing. Paxton was needed at the clinic. There was more pressure than ever for him to take over his father's practice and place on the clinic board. Paxton could see the future mapped out for him.

"Not to pry but you said there was no wife or girlfriend but I saw something about a wedding."

He guessed he owed her some explanation. She had answered his questions. Even the personal ones. "I no longer have a fiancée. There was no wedding."

"I'm sorry."

"I'm not. In hindsight, it was something my parents wanted more than me. We'd been friends for a long time and it was more about it being time to marry than about love." At least he'd come to that conclusion on the long drive west.

His phone rang. He looked at it. He sighed. It was his father. "Excuse me a sec. I need to get this," he said to Lauren. He answered as he walked toward his bedroom. "Hi, Dad."

"How're things going out there?" For once his father sounded genuinely interested.

Paxton told him a little about a couple of cases he'd seen.

"That sounds good, but you know you have patients here as well who depend on you."

Here it goes.

"I know that but I'm in Last Stop for now."

"Son, you need to think about what you're doing. Your patients will find another doctor if you stay away too long. Can't they get someone so you can come back sooner? You're needed at the board meeting next week. The least you could do is be home for Christmas. Your mother—"

Paxton had heard all of this he wanted. "Dad, I've got to go. I have a patient to see. I'll talk to you later. Bye."

He returned to the kitchen.

Lauren gave him a questioning look. "Everything okay?"

"Yeah. Just my father checking in." Paxton glanced at his watch. "Before we get back to work, do you think you could get Mr. Gerhart's phone number for me? Discreetly?"

"I can do that." Concern filled her eyes. "Is there something seriously wrong?"

It wouldn't hurt for her to know. Lauren was a professional. She would keep the secret. "It doesn't appear to be the bladder infection I suspected. I need to do an exam for an enlarged prostate. At his age... He seemed like a really private man and I don't want to broadcast he might have a problem."

Her mouth went into a thin line. "I appreciate that. He's one of those men's men who doesn't like to show weakness."

"I think most of us are." Or at least he had been before Gabriella had cut him down to size in that area. His ego had definitely taken a hit.

They finished their meals and Lauren took their plates to the dishwasher. "I'll get that number for you."

Paxton watched the gentle sway of her hips, encased in tight jeans again, as she walked away. Her hair was tied back and his fingers itched to pull her ponytail down and see it cascade around her shoulders. Why did he find her so alluring? Maybe it was because she knew him only as himself and not the Boston socialite whose fiancée had all but left him at the altar.

His parents had made it clear his recent decision to leave town reflected negatively on the family. They believed he should have forgiven Gabriella and moved on. For him loyalty was a basic building block of a relationship. One he wasn't willing or going to compromise on, not even to make his parents happy.

Paxton headed for his office, wanting to check on the latest lab results.

A few minutes later Lauren handed him a slip of paper. "Here's Mr. Gerhart's number."

Mr. Gerhart answered on the second ring. Paxton explained the situation and asked the man to come in. He refused. Paxton told him he would come to him then and that what was going on would remain between the two of them. Mr. Gerhart agreed. Paxton finished with, "Okay, I'll see you in fifteen minutes."

Paxton went in search of Lauren. He found her in the small closet where he planned to put the lab. She was pulling a box by her fingertips off an upper shelf. "Hey, let me get that for you."

The box tilted to one side and Paxton hurried to put a hand up to stop it from falling on her. Lauren jerked away as he grabbed the box. He placed it on a lower shelf and turned to face her. Her eyes were wide as she stared at him. Electricity arced between them.

She appeared ready to run. Did the fear he might kiss her have her that skittish? Making her afraid of him had not been his intention.

In an attempt to calm her he asked, "Hey, what's so important in this box that you'd be willing to bring it down on your head?"

"Christmas decorations."

His mouth fell open. That was the last thing he'd expected her to answer. She'd caught him completely by surprise.

"You know—those things that shine and twinkle, that you put up once a year."

Her sassy tone made him grin. "Yeah, I know what they are. I just hadn't thought about them being here." He took the box, stepped out into the kitchen and set it on one of the chairs.

Lauren joined him.

"I got Mr. Gerhart on the phone. The conversation was short and to the point but he agreed to see me and I have to go to him. I'm headed out now. I'll see any patient who comes in just as soon as I return. Can you tell me where he lives?"

"Out off the Lippscomb Highway. Turn at the second road. Third farm on the left. Red barn."

"Sounds doable. After I get back I thought I'd drive to Lippscomb and get that shopping done. I know it's your afternoon off, but I'd appreciate you showing me where to go."

For a second, he was afraid she was going to turn him down, but she shrugged. "I guess I could, but Shawn will have to go with us."

Outside seeing children occasionally in his practice, he hadn't been around them much. He liked them well enough but had never spent an afternoon with one. "That shouldn't be a problem."

She gave him a thoughtful look for a moment as if she sensed his uncertainty. "I'll go pick him up and be waiting here when you get back."

"Sounds like a plan. Wish me luck with Mr. Gerhart." Paxton started toward the back door.

She grinned. "You'll need it."

"Thanks for the encouragement," he called over his shoulder as he left. It was nice to share a conversation with a woman who made him smile when he went out the door. Whenever he'd left Gabriella, she had been complaining or telling him what social engagement she had decided they would attend next. Why hadn't he noticed that before now?

CHAPTER FIVE

PAXTON ENTERED THE kitchen through the back door. Lauren was at the kitchen table, putting an ornament on a miniature tree sitting on the table. She'd changed clothes and was now wearing a heavy-knit sweater in green with a large collar over black jeans. Her cowboy boots had been replaced by some dressier boots. She looked fashionable and sexy at the same time.

He grinned. "Success."

She stopped what she was doing and looked at him. "Really? How did you manage that?"

He put his bag on a chair and pulled his gloves off, dropping them on the table. "I can't give away my trade secrets." He couldn't help but be proud of himself.

"What did you do? Threaten to tell his wife? Make him come here? Say you would tell everyone in town?"

"Let's just say I put it in terms a man can understand." He removed his coat.

"I have to say I'm impressed. Not even Dr. Barden managed to get him to see him. House call or not. You're my hero."

Her hero? He liked the sound of that. It was like balm to his bruised ego. Paxton's grin grew into a full smile. "Thanks." His attention turned to the table. "What have you been up to here?"

"Just putting up Christmas decorations."

He gave the tree a look. "You didn't have to do that for me."

"Well, with the exception of this tree, it's more for the patients." She hung the last ornament.

"Mommy?"

Paxton's head swung to the door of his bedroom. A little boy with dark hair and dressed in navy overalls came toddling out.

"Hey, there, honey." Lauren swooped Shawn up into her arms and pulled him to her chest for a hug. She turned to Paxton. "I hope you don't mind, I put him down for a nap on a pallet in your room. Less draft."

"No, I don't mind."

"Shawn—" Lauren looked at the boy with such love and devotion "—this is Dr. Samuels."

"That's a mouthful for a little boy. Make it Paxton." The look he received from Lauren made him think he'd said something wonderful.

"Max," Shawn said.

"Pax," he said, and Lauren shook her head and laughed. "How old is he?" Paxton asked. He'd always been ambivalent about children. With the family he'd grown up in he wasn't sure he really wanted any. He didn't want the pressure he felt to rub off on his own kids.

"Two and a half. I'll get Shawn changed and we'll head to Lippscomb." She went into his room.

Paxton stepped to the door, leaned against the doorpost and watched as she changed Shawn's diaper with the same efficiency she did everything. As she worked she spoke to the boy, making him giggle.

Lauren came to Paxton and held Shawn out to him. "If you'll hold him a sec, I can get his diaper bag together."

Paxton hesitated. He didn't make a habit of holding children. When Shawn reached for him Paxton took him, holding him out from his body.

"If you hold him a little closer it would be easier." Lauren picked up a bag with tractors on the cover and stuffed some items in it.

"Max," Shawn repeated with a grin.

Lauren laughed. "You may get another name."

"Uh…yeah, I can tell that." He handed Shawn back to her with some relief.

In the kitchen, Lauren bundled the boy into a coat and hat. While she did that, Paxton put his own coat on. Lauren handed Shawn to him again. It was as if she thought everyone was comfortable holding a baby. She shrugged into her coat, which had been hanging on one of the chairs. With that done, she reached for Shawn, who happily went back to her. Paxton was glad to have her take him. Lauren pulled the bag up over her shoulder with the ease of someone who had juggled it all before.

At the back door, she said, "I'll drive. Shawn's car seat is already in the truck. Your fancy sports car wasn't made with babies in mind."

Paxton went to the passenger seat while Lauren strapped Shawn into his seat in the back before she slid behind the steering wheel. He was used to doing the driving, was usually the one in control. Here he was again at her mercy.

They were on the outskirts of town when he asked, "So do you have a place in mind where I can get some clothes?"

"I know just the place. They should have everything you need." She picked up the speed.

"Good. I don't want to have to do this again."

"Not a shopper?"

"No. I usually order what I need. My doorman sees to my returns."

"Doorman, huh?" She glanced at him. "Why am I not surprised?"

"What's that supposed to mean?" She made it sound like he was a criminal.

"You just strike me as a man who's used to doing the everyday things in the simplest way."

At least that was a step above saying he was too lazy to do for himself. He watched her. She had her hair down but pinned back on one side so that her pert nose was clearly visible. The sunlight reflected off her soft skin, giving her a healthy glow. She was nothing like the make-up-dependent women he was familiar with.

Shawn squealed, jolting him out of his thoughts.

"We're almost there, sweetheart. I know you're ready to get out of that seat." Lauren reached back and shook Shawn's chair. He quieted for a minute then started up again. She asked Paxton, "Would you mind handing him that toy that's on the seat?"

Paxton twisted in the seat, found the truck and gave it to Shawn, who promptly threw it on the floor. This could be one of the reasons he had never shown much interest in children. Reaching around as far as he could, bringing him in contact with Lauren's shoulder, he grabbed the toy. Lauren's sharp intake of breath didn't miss his attention. Paxton handed the truck to the boy. "Here you go."

Shawn threw the truck again.

"Stop that, Shawn!" Lauren glared back at him.

Shawn continued to play the game, giggling and grinning each time he dropped the toy. Lauren finally pulled into a parking space in front of a building. Paxton was relieved—he hadn't been having as much fun with that game as Shawn had been.

They were in front of a department store on the main street in Lippscomb. "I'll need to get Shawn in the stroller then I'll be on in."

"I'll get the stroller." Paxton had seen it in the back of the truck when he'd gotten in. He went to the tailgate, released it and lifted the folded stroller out. He attempted to unfold it. It released part of the way but refused to lock into place.

"You have to pull up on the red button while pulling on the handle to get it to lock into place," Lauren called.

It took him a couple of seconds to locate the button. He tried again. Nothing. He'd seen surgeries less complicated than dealing with a stroller. Paxton was still working with it when Lauren joined him with Shawn in her arms.

He gave her a contrite look.

She grinned. "I'll admit it's not that easy."

He didn't like having his vulnerability show. He couldn't look like less of a man because of a stroller. At least she wasn't laughing at him. "Does this thing require an engineering degree to work it?"

"No, but it can be contrary."

Lauren handed him Shawn, which was the lesser of two evils at this point. Shawn patted Paxton's face as if they were new best friends. Lauren soon had the stroller open and was reaching for her son. With the efficiency of a mother who had done the job more than once, she had the boy strapped in and ready to go. She pushed the stroller toward the double glass doors.

Paxton followed, feeling defeated. He'd questioned having children and the ride to Lippscomb with Shawn had confirmed it. He should think long and hard about being a parent. He held the door open for Shawn and Lauren to enter.

Lauren said as she passed him and entered the store, "You're not the first to have a problem with that stroller. You should have seen me the first time."

That did make him feel a little better.

Inside she stopped and waved a hand in the direction of the right side of the store. "You should find what you need over there. Shawn and I are going to go over here—" she indicated the other side of the store "—to see if we can find something to wear for the community Christmas party."

"What's that?"

She gave him an odd look. "You know, where all the town comes together for dinner and a dance."

Paxton shrugged. "I've never been to something like that." He'd attended plenty of country club dances but never one where an entire community was invited.

"It's the best event of the year. Great food, kids running around and a couple of the local guys making up a band. It's so much fun. Really puts you in the Christmas spirit."

Paxton wasn't sure that or anything else would put

him in the spirit. He'd never been big on Christmas or family get-togethers. And after his non-wedding he didn't care about them. He wasn't feeling warm and fuzzy about anything these days.

"Everyone is welcome. You need to plan to come. It would be a great way to meet everyone."

He shook his head. "I don't know. I'm not much on parties."

He started off toward the men's clothing. Years of required country club parties and social "must-dos" had him eager to stay away from anything that resembled one. At least if he did decide to go it would be because he wanted to, not because he was pressured into it. Not unlike what he felt when one of his parents called now.

Going to the men's department, he picked up a couple of pairs of slacks and some denim shirts but he made a point to avoid the Western-cut ones. He didn't see them as his style. Finding the socks, Paxton picked out a number of pairs of thick ones. The ties hung close by. There was a red one with reindeer heads on it. For some reason he felt daring. He didn't know where he would wear it but it was something his mother would frown on and that was enough. Conservative ties and suits had been the norm for him for so long it felt good to branch out.

He was checking out his purchases at the back of the store when Lauren walked up. She had some red fabric over her arm and a child's outfit hanging on the stroller handle. "I see you found something."

She put the clothing on the counter for the woman to ring up. "Yeah, we don't get many reasons for dressy events around here so I'm making the most of it."

Unlike the world he'd left, where his hand-tailored tuxedo hung in his closet.

"So when we do, everyone makes the most of it." She smiled. "And it's Christmastime."

She made her purchases and they returned to the car. As she put Shawn in his car seat Paxton made a show of folding and putting the stroller in the truck. It turned out it was much easier to close than to open. Puffed with pride, he got into the passenger seat.

Lauren looked at him with a grin on her lips. "Feeling pretty good about yourself, aren't you?"

His chin went high. "Yes, I am."

She giggled. A real giggle. He hadn't heard a sound like that in years. One that rang of sincerity. Women around him had made a noise like a giggle as a way of getting their way, but Lauren's was one of pure pleasure. It was a sound he wanted to experience again.

As she backed out of the parking space she asked, "Do you mind if we stop by the feed store? My father needs me to pick up a couple of bags of feed for a calf that's not eating well."

"Sure. That's fine with me."

Lauren drove out of town the way they had come. They were almost to the town limits when she pulled into a gravel lot. They faced a low building that was set well off the road and had a loading dock running across the front of it. Pickup trucks of all makes and models, including a number with stock trailers attached, were parked in the lot.

Pulling close to a ramp, she said, "This is one of the best places in town. They have everything you need from feed, to clothing, to house goods. One-stop shopping."

"So why didn't we come here first?"

She studied him up and down, wrinkled her nose and said, "Not your style. And I'd been thinking about the dress I bought."

"I get it. We were really shopping for you," he teased.

"Maybe a little bit."

Paxton enjoyed their easy banter. He'd had too little of that in his life. Lauren had a quick wit. It was refreshing to have a woman be completely honest with him.

Climbing out of the truck, he quickly had the stroller out and ready by the time Lauren had Shawn in her arms.

"Ever been to a Feed and Seed before?" Lauren asked as she put Shawn in the stroller.

"No."

"You're in for a treat." She pushed the stroller up the ramp. "This was my favorite place to come as a child. Shawn already loves it."

Paxton joined her as they walked past a large open roller door. She continued down the dock to the double glass entrance. He held a door wide for her while she maneuvered Shawn inside.

Lauren was right. He had never been any place like it. There were work clothes, boots and hats, camping equipment, guns, feed bins for any size animal, horse tack and garden tools. He could hardly keep up with Lauren for looking around at stuff he would have no idea how to find in Boston.

She headed straight down the center aisle to the

back of the store. There he saw a counter behind which stood a bearded man wearing a flannel shirt. A number of other men mingled nearby, talking to one another or just drinking from mugs. All of them wore cowboy hats, heavy coats and well-worn cowboy boots. Each man either spoke, nodded or tipped their hat to Lauren as she approached.

"Hey, Joe," she said to the man behind the counter. "Can I get a couple of twenty-five-pound bags of that special calf mix for Dad?"

The man smiled at her. "Sure. I'll be right out with it."

"Just put it on Dad's tab," she called to his back.

Paxton had wandered to a shelf filled with all types of knives. She came over to him. "Tab?" Paxton questioned. "People still do that?"

She looked surprised at the question and nodded. "Yep, people still do that. Dad pays his off on the first of the month."

Where he came from nobody would even consider running a tab for someone. That kind of trust had long gone. He liked the idea that people in the area did things based on faith. He had certainly had his shaken by Gabriella and his parents.

By the time they had arrived back at the truck a couple of strapping young men arrived with a bag apiece over their shoulders.

"Just put it in the back," Lauren told them as she strapped a wiggling Shawn into his seat. Paxton stowed the stroller. A strange sense of accomplishment came over him for having mastered it.

Lauren waved. "Thanks, guys."

They were leaving the parking lot when Paxton

asked, "Before we head back, why don't we get some dinner? I owe you for the pizza and breakfast the other day."

She pulled onto the highway. "I appreciate the offer but I can't. I get too little time with Shawn as it is and Wednesday night is our family time. I really try to protect it."

Was she kidding? Family time? What he knew about family time was rushing to get in the car to head to a social event his mother said they all must attend. Actually spending real time listening and talking and finding out who he really was his parents had never done. Maybe they didn't want to know. "Maybe next time."

Their trip home consisted of mostly Lauren singing or talking to Shawn. She was a good mother who obviously loved her child dearly. They were almost at Last Stop when the boy nodded off to sleep.

"Well, you'll at least get a mile or two of peace." Lauren laughed.

"It hasn't been that bad." To his surprise, it hadn't. "He seems like a nice kid."

"Yeah, he is. I rather like him." She looked into the rear-view mirror with a slight smile on her lips and love shining in her eyes.

What would it be like to have someone like Lauren look at him with such love and devotion? He'd never seen that in Gabriella and he'd been planning to marry her! What had he been thinking? How had he let his parents' expectations control his life so much? He was a grown man, working in a field of responsibility and he'd let others lead him around by the nose. Why?

Because he'd been brought up to honor his family

heritage, because he loved his parents and wanted to make them happy. Because he'd never really thought about what he wanted. What would make him happy. He knew clearly one thing he didn't want, to be married to someone just because it was the right thing to do.

He'd already learned more about himself in less than a week while being around Lauren and living in Last Stop than he had in years of living his other life.

A few minutes later Lauren pulled into the clinic drive. "I appreciate you taking me along today." He gathered his packages.

"Not a problem. I'll see you in the morning."

Paxton watched her back out. He didn't like the feeling of being left behind.

CHAPTER SIX

THE NEXT TWO days at the clinic passed for Paxton much the same as the others, minus another tractor accident. He and Lauren were kept busy tending patients. Lewis and Mr. Thompson came in for their checkups. Both again expressed their gratitude.

Friday evening Lauren announced with a wave, "See you Monday morning."

Paxton had an unshakable sensation of being left behind again, but he needed the time to think. He'd run to Last Stop in the heat of the moment, to put distance between him and the shambles of his life in Boston, but he couldn't hide forever.

This was only a temporary reprieve from his career and responsibilities in Boston. He had a practice, positions on committees and people who expected results from him. With his father's illness, the duties had grown. While in Last Stop he had to make some positive decisions regarding his life, his future.

That evening, he had dinner in front of the TV. He couldn't remember the last time he'd not had plans for the weekend. The freedom he was discovering in Last Stop had a healthy appeal.

Though Saturday morning was overcast and gray

he went out anyway, intent on exploring. He drove along each street. It didn't take him long to see the entire town because it was only six blocks long and four wide. He had no idea where Lauren lived but he'd secretly hoped he might run into her. By the time he'd seen everything it was close enough to lunchtime that he stopped in at the café on Main Street.

"Hi, Dr. Samuels."

His waitress turned out to be Margie, who'd come in with the burned hand.

"Well, hi. How's your hand?"

She waved it at him. "I'm waiting tables until it gets better."

"Good. Are you keeping it dry and clean?"

She nodded. "Just like you told me. So, what can I get you?"

"I'd like the soup of the day and a BLT." Paxton took a seat at one of the tables.

While he ate, more than one person stopped and welcomed him to town. If he had been out for a meal in Boston no one would have looked him in the eye as they walked past, much less said hi. Here he felt appreciated. Another essential he lacked in his life.

Returning home, he checked lab results, but there was nothing that couldn't be taken care of on Monday. By mid-afternoon he was bored. Eager to start on the lab, he went searching for tools. Finding them under the kitchen sink, he proceeded to tear out the shelves on one side of the closet.

It was dusk when he started hauling them out to the backyard and heard the sounds of a band tuning up. It seemed to be coming from the direction of the high school he'd passed that morning. He looked around the house. Warmly dressed people were walking toward Main Street.

What's going on?

He wanted to find out. Washing up quickly, he grabbed his coat, gloves and beanie. He walked the block to where people were gathering along the street. Stopping beside a woman holding a child's hand, he asked, "What's happening?"

"Santa is coming," the little girl said, her face alight with excitement.

Her mother offered, "It's the annual Christmas parade. It starts in a few minutes."

Paxton nodded. "Oh." When was the last time he'd been to a Christmas parade? Or any parade, for that matter? His parents hadn't had time for that sort of thing.

Lewis, grinning and flanked by his grandfather, came up to Paxton. "Hi, Doc."

"Hey, Lewis. Nice to see you again. Mr. Gerhart." Paxton extended his hand.

The older man accepted it.

"You know my grandfather?" Lewis glanced curiously from one to the other.

"Uh, we met the other day." Paxton covered the best he could.

"Pops, I see someone I know. I'll see you later." Lewis patted his grandfather on the shoulder and without a backward glance headed straight for a teenage girl.

"So, how're you doing, Mr. Gerhart?" Paxton said, for the man's ears only.

"Better. Thanks for not saying anything in front of Lewis."

"Not a problem."

The noise of marching band instruments starting into a Christmas carol filled the air. Paxton looked up the street toward the sound and spied Lauren, with Shawn on her hip. She wore the white coat she'd had on the first night they'd met. Her hood was over her head and pulled tight around her face. She was what he imagined a snow nymph would look like. Tiny, in white, with large expressive eyes. She lifted a mitten-covered hand in a small wave of acknowledgment.

"Mr. Gerhart, I see my nurse over there. I need to speak to her."

The older man gave him a wise, knowing look and a nod.

The band was coming down the street in formation just as Paxton jogged across the street. He squeezed in next to Lauren. "Hey."

She smiled. "Hey, yourself."

Paxton leaned in close so she could hear over the band. "Why didn't you tell me about this?"

"You didn't seem interested in the community dinner and dance so I thought you wouldn't be interested in this."

"Point taken."

"I saw you talking to your new best friend, Mr. Gerhart. Interested in getting anything off your chest?" Her look didn't waver.

"Nope." He smiled at her frustrated expression. "Patient-doctor privilege."

"You know I can keep a secret."

Paxton moved his face closer and whispered in her ear. "So can I."

"Funny."

The passing band made hearing difficult after that. It consisted of only ten people and was led by two young girls carrying a banner with "Merry Christmas" in big letters surrounded by glitter. Behind them was a pickup truck filled with cheerleaders waving their pom-poms. The crowd called out names and they responded with smiles and waves. It was followed by a convertible car with a man and woman waving from the back seat.

Paxton gave Lauren a quizzical look.

"The mayor and his wife."

They were followed by a tractor pulling a trailer loaded with a group of girls dressed in red cowboy hats, white shirts and full red skirts. They each waved to the crowd and threw candy to the kids. Again Paxton looked at Lauren.

"The Christmas Queen and her court."

"Oh." Interesting.

"I was the queen one year."

"I'm not surprised. You're pretty enough to be one." That was true but he shouldn't have said it out loud.

Lauren looked as shocked as he felt. Her eyes shone as she said, "Thank you."

Another couple of floats came by.

Lauren shifted Shawn to her other hip, putting him between them. A minute later another large tractor with a trailer attached came their way. Sitting on hay bales surrounded by presents was Santa Claus.

The crowd closed in on them. Lauren lifted Shawn to shoulder level. There was no way she would be able to hold him like that for long. Paxton took him from her and set Shawn on his shoulders.

Lauren looked at him in wonder and then appreciation. The boy fussed a little at Paxton's handling but settled when Lauren said, "Shawn, look. There's Santa Claus."

Apparently Shawn hadn't looked in the direction she had wanted him to so Lauren wrapped her fingers around Paxton's arm and pulled close. "See, honey, there he is." She pointed to the road but she was watching Shawn, her face glowing with pure pleasure.

Paxton had never been a part of this type of parental moment yet it gave him a contented feeling deep inside, as if he were part of something special. That he somehow belonged. He looked at the people around him and across the street. This was a genuinely close-knit community. People knew each other, enjoyed the simple things in life and understood why that simplicity was important. Like having your child see Santa in a parade.

Big snowflakes started falling. Even to his jaded heart it was a magical moment.

Paxton anticipated that everyone would disperse in different directions when the parade was over. Instead, they all headed down the street in the same direction. "Where's everyone going?"

"To the church for hot chocolate. Wanna come?" Lauren's inviting grin made the decision for him.

He brought Shawn down into his arms. "Why not?"

Shawn wiggled and reached out for Lauren. Paxton handed him over. They followed the crowd.

Someone began to sing "We Wish You a Merry Christmas." The song grew in volume as everyone joined in, all headed to the white clapboard building with the tall steeple on the next block.

He and Lauren followed the line into a side door

of the building. In the anteroom, they pulled off their caps and gloves. They were standing in the doorway, waiting to enter the crowded fellowship hall, when a girl of about ten years old came running up and slid to a stop.

She pointed above their heads and shouted, "They're under the mistletoe! They have to kiss!"

Virtually everyone turned to look at him and Lauren. Every expression clearly asked, *Well, are you going to kiss her?*

Paxton had been brought up to do what was expected of him. What made this situation special was his eagerness to comply.

Lauren's eyelids slowly lowered as he leaned in to find her lips. They were cool from having been outside, yet lush and smooth. Perfect. It was a chaste kiss as kisses went yet an electric jolt, warming him from the core out, shot through him.

Shawn wiggled in Lauren's arms. The kiss was almost over before it began. A few people snickered while others clapped but the moment was soon forgotten as the line formed to accept hot chocolate in plastic cups from women who were undoubtedly matriarchs of Last Stop. For Paxton the kiss lingered on his tingling lips. It hadn't been enough.

They mingled with the crowd. Lauren introduced a number of people to him and he was able to speak to some he'd seen during the week.

Soon Shawn yawned and Lauren announced it was time for her to go. They all bundled up again and headed out into the snowy night.

"May I walk you home or to your truck?" Paxton asked with confidence he didn't feel. The possibility she might say no was a bit unsettling. "I have no idea where you go after work," he quickly added, and for some reason he really wanted to know.

"Thanks, but neither are necessary. I just live a couple of blocks from here. Down that way." She pointed in the opposite direction from the one they had come. "I assure you I'll be fine."

He must have passed her house in his wanderings earlier in the day and not known it. "Just the same, I'll walk you home. I was taught to be a gentleman and to see that a lady gets home safely."

She chuckled. "I've never had anyone say that to me before."

"You should have."

Lauren gave him a speculative look then started down the sidewalk. "Well, if you insist."

"I do. And I insist you let me carry Shawn." Paxton reached for Shawn, who had fallen asleep. "He has to be heavy."

She gave her son up. Somehow having Lauren next to him as they walked through the night gave him a sense of peace he'd not known in a long time, if ever. The fact she had a child, he wasn't so sure about.

"This is me," Lauren said in front of a tiny clapboard house with a porch across the front. A single light glowed in the window of what had to be her living room.

"I'll take him now." She reached for Shawn.

"I've got him. Show me where to put him." Paxton walked toward the front door. By the time he climbed the three steps Lauren had the door open for him to enter. He stepped into her small living area. A floral sofa faced the window, an armchair filled in one corner. The TV took another and toys were everywhere.

"Down this way." Lauren flipped on a light in the hall.

Paxton trailed after her to a room decorated in cowboys and horses. A low bed was stationed in the corner. He laid Shawn on it. Standing back, he watched Lauren remove her son's jacket and shoes.

"Tonight it won't hurt for him to sleep in his clothes," she whispered, before kissing Shawn on the forehead. She pulled the door partially closed behind her as they moved out into the hall. "Thanks for carrying him home. He's getting to be a heavy load."

"Not a problem." Paxton watched her for a moment, sort of hoping she'd ask him to stay for a while. When she didn't he said, "Well, I'd better go." It took willpower to conceal his disappointment.

She followed him to the front door. There he turned. "You know, I've been thinking about that kiss and I believe I can do a better job."

"Oh?"

He cupped her cheeks then covered her mouth with his. Her full lips pillowed his. There was a trembling hesitation before her hands slid up over his shoulders and around his neck. Her fingers tangled in his hair, nudging his head closer. His hands moved to her waist and pulled her against him. Paxton took the kiss deeper. She joined him in freefall.

Moments later he pulled back, breathless. "I think that was much better."

"Uh-huh," she said softly.

Lauren's eyes were glossy, her plump lips rosy. The temptation to kiss her again grew but if he gave in to it, he'd press for more, much more. She was too tantalizing for her own good but she didn't deserve being a rebound woman. His life was so screwed up he'd run away from it. He didn't have the right to involve her in the mess.

He stepped out the door. His voice hoarse with desire, he said, "'Night, Lauren."

An intense driving need made his heart race and held him balanced on the edge of reason. He'd never experienced this with Gabriella. Only with Lauren had he felt this new level of desire. He feared it couldn't be eased except by having her.

Doing his best to get his body under control, Paxton watched Lauren slowly close the door between them. The biting cold was welcome. It cooled his libido enough to stop him from knocking on her door.

Monday morning Lauren's body was still humming from Paxton's kiss. She had to continually remind herself that it meant nothing. It had been the mistletoe. Or him proving a point. Nothing special.

Yet her body refused to accept that. Their kiss *had* been special to her. Her toes had curled and she'd been speechless afterward. When she'd looked into Paxton's eyes there had been raw desire in their depths. It called to her even now. The second his lips had touched hers she'd lost her ability to think. What she'd had with Mark had been good but it had been easy, natural. With Paxton she felt unsure, oversensitive, an erotic excitement that was as frightening as it was new. It was as if she was walking too close to the edge of a cliff but couldn't stop herself from leaning forward to look over. It was both exhilarating and terrifying.

Was history repeating itself? Was she being swept into something where hurt would be the only outcome? It would be best if she and Paxton stayed at arm's length but she wasn't even sure she could do that. Caution should be her standard.

After dropping Shawn off at the babysitter's for the day, she drove to the clinic with some trepidation and hot anticipation. Would Paxton mention their kiss? Try to do it again? Did she want him to?

Lauren entered through the front door, consciously respecting his personal space in the back. She was surprised not to find him in the office, checking lab results. After storing her coat and purse, she still hadn't seen or heard him. Was he still asleep?

"Paxton," she called as she went down the hall.

"Hey," came faintly from the back.

He wasn't in the kitchen.

"In here."

He was in the closet. Lauren hesitated at the door. She wasn't ready to be in such close quarters with Paxton again. He wore a soft-looking flannel shirt, jeans and leather shoes. The attire made him appear relaxed, as if he belonged. Not the uptight, big-city doctor who didn't want to admit he needed her help who she'd met a week earlier. He was becoming more attractive by the day.

She made an effort to focus on the closet structure instead of him. "Hey, you've been busy."

"Yep." He looked at her from where he sat at the workbench. "I had some time on my hands this weekend so I decided to get started."

"I see that. Even painted, I see." Had he been thinking about their kiss, reliving it over and over, while he'd worked? Now she was thinking like a high-school girl in the throes of her first crush. The kiss hadn't been that big a deal for him, she was sure.

"I got that done yesterday," he was saying. "Everything's ready for the equipment. That should be here sometime today. All I need is the electric connection. I spoke to Mr. Gerhart yesterday and he volunteered an electrician guy to do it. He should be here any minute."

There was a ring at the front door.

"I'll get that. It may be a patient." She turned to go.

"Hey, Lauren."

"Yeah?"

"It's nice to see you." He watched her as if judging her reaction, as if he was unsure of what it might be.

Warmth flowed through her like the first rays of sun after snow. "It's nice to see you too."

"Anyone here?" came a deep, gravelly voice.

"Coming," Lauren called back.

The voice belonged to Mr. Adamson, the electrician. Lauren sent him back to Paxton when a patient arrived. She had barely gotten the patient to the exam room when Paxton showed up and went to work.

The rest of the day was spent caring for minor illnesses and injuries. Late that afternoon a delivery truck arrived and left several boxes in the waiting room. Paxton was visibly excited to see them. As soon as the last patient left he started opening the largest.

Disappointment doused Lauren, almost extinguishing the hope she'd been harboring, when Paxton barely acknowledged she was leaving for the day. The next day was the same. Paxton was in his new lab every second he had between patients. Her hope he'd put any emotional emphasis on their kiss was dashed. As far as she could tell, he didn't even know she was there.

She did have to give him credit for putting in the lab. Even though he wouldn't be there but for a few more weeks he was making a lasting difference in the lives of Last Stop. He had already made a couple of diagnoses that would have had to wait longer if it hadn't been for the lab on site. Paxton was a good man.

By Wednesday at noon, when they closed for the day, she was ready to spend the afternoon with Shawn and forget about any emotions Paxton roused in her. Her plans were for her and Shawn to have some fun and decorate their Christmas tree. She went in search of Paxton to tell him she was leaving.

"No, Mom, I'll be home before New Year." Paxton's voice carried into the kitchen from the lab.

He was on the phone. She'd wait a second for him to finish his call.

Then he said, "Yes, I understand that Dad needs me. I will be home in two weeks. I've made a commitment here. I have to honor it. I can't just up and leave."

Lauren shouldn't be eavesdropping but she couldn't make herself move.

Paxton continued, "No. There's not another doctor who can handle things here. I'll be back as soon as I can. If you have something else you'd like to talk about then I'll be glad to listen but if not I have to go."

He didn't say anything for a minute and Lauren stepped into the doorway, thinking he was off the phone.

"Yes, Mother, I know where my place is. I understand my position and I know how ill Dad is. I get it. Please tell Dad to take care of himself. I'll talk to you soon." With that Paxton dropped his phone onto the bench.

"Everything okay?" Lauren asked softly.

Paxton whirled around. "Uh, yeah. You know, same old family drama."

Lauren watched him a moment. Why did she think there was more to it? What was the deal with his parents anyway? "We all have it sometime. I just wanted to let you know I was leaving."

"Where're you going?"

He really had his mind in another place. "It's our half-day today."

"Yeah, that's right, it is." He turned back to what he was doing in the lab. "See you later."

She was tempted to ask him more about the call from his mother but if the tension showing in his shoulders was any indication he wasn't going to talk to her about it.

A couple of hours later she was just getting ready to start with the tree decorations when there was a knock at her door. Opening it, she found Paxton standing on the porch with an aluminum casserole pan in his hands.

"Hey, I thought if I brought dinner you might share it with me."

"What, you're not eating in your new lab?"

He gave her a wry smile. "I do get tunnel vision when I start a new project but I'm tired of eating alone. I thought I'd take a chance and see if you'd take pity on me."

"It depends on what kind of casserole you have there," she replied in a teasing tone, keeping the thrill that went through her that he was on her doorstep to herself.

He frowned down at it. "I think it's chicken and rice."

"Okay. That sounds good. Come on in." She took the aluminum foil dish from him.

Paxton followed Lauren down the hall. Pictures of happy people filled the walls. Those must be her family members.

She led him all the way to the back where the kitchen was located. It was much like his at the clinic. The kitchen was sunshine yellow with orange accents. Despite the house being small, it had a warm, lived-in atmosphere. Her home revealed hidden aspects of Lauren's personality he'd never have suspected had he not acted on his need for company.

She turned on the oven and slid the casserole inside.

He hadn't seen or heard her son. Was there a chance he had her to himself?

"Where's Shawn?"

"He's taking a nap," she answered with smile.

He wasn't so sure that Shawn liked him but, then again, he wouldn't be around long enough for it to really matter. The only problem was that he liked Shawn's mother, but he wasn't sure about taking on a child anyway. That had never been in his plans.

"It's about time for him to get up," Lauren continued. "We're going to decorate the tree." As she headed to the front of the house she said over her slender shoulder, "I still need to get the lights on before he wakes up. There's only so much that you can do with a two-year-old and a Christmas tree, but I'm carrying on a family tradition, creating family memories."

Paxton grinned. Lauren sure was chatty. Was she nervous about him being there? He rather liked the thought his presence had her a little off center.

He joined her in the living room to see an artificial tree standing in the middle of it. Family memories weren't something Paxton had many of, positive ones anyway. Even when his family did, or had done, something together he'd always felt like he was an outsider. Didn't quite measure up to his family's expectations. There was always the burden to do as his parents wanted.

"Here, you can get started with these." Lauren reached for a strand of lights.

Paxton took them from her and studied them. He looked up to find her watching him.

"Is something wrong?"

"No. I have just never done this before." Paxton hated to admit that.

"You have never put or seen Christmas lights hung on a tree?" Her expression made him feel like he was from another planet.

He shook his head. "Afraid not. The housekeeper always took care of that." Even to him that sounded sad.

"Then you'll learn something new tonight," was her cheerful response. "Take this end and just start at the top and go around and around until you get to the bottom. I'll keep them untangled back here."

Paxton followed her directions, placing the lights in among the branches.

"My parents, my brother and I all trimmed the tree together," she volunteered with a happy face as they worked in tandem. "I want to give Shawn the same memories."

With the lights completed, Lauren turned to a box and opened it. "I love the ornaments. Each one brings back a memory."

She glanced at him. "I guess you've never hung decorations either."

He winced and shook his head. "No."

"Then you'll get to make a memory tonight in addition to learning something. So, if you didn't decorate a tree, what kind of family traditions at Christmas do you have?"

"We've always gone to the country club for Christmas Eve dinner, then opened presents at ten o'clock sharp."

"That's it?" She sounded disappointed.

"I went to my room to play with whatever toys I got. My father often had to go to the hospital and my mother would rest in her room. Holidays have always been quiet at my house."

"Mommy?" A call came from down the hall.

"Now the fun begins." Lauren had a skip in her step and a smile on her face as she left the room. She soon returned with Shawn in her arms.

"Shawn, look who's here," Lauren said.

The boy gave him a solemn look and rubbed his eyes.

"Hi, Shawn," Paxton offered.

"Are you ready to decorate the tree?" Lauren asked Shawn with enthusiasm, giving him a kiss on the cheek then setting him on his feet.

She went to the box of ornaments and pulled out a fat Santa.

"Would you like to put it on the tree?" Lauren motioned and Shawn went over to the tree. Guiding his hand, she helped the boy hang the red ball-shaped figurine. "Now we must be careful not to touch it once it's on the tree."

She picked out another ornament, a bell this time, and did the same thing. Shawn giggled when it rang. Paxton couldn't keep the smile off his face. Even with his jaded background he had to allow that Shawn was a lucky child to have such a loving mother who wanted him to grow up with happy memories.

Paxton sensed Lauren's pleased gaze on him just before she asked, "Would you do the ones up high?"

"I guess I could do that."

Lauren handed him an ornament by the hanger. "All you have to do is put this little hook over the branch."

His eyes narrowed. With sarcasm dripping from his words, he informed her, "I think I can handle it."

Her eyes were alight with mischief. "I do too."

Once he did it, Paxton found he rather enjoyed the simple task.

When they finished Lauren picked up Shawn and walked to the light switch and turned it off. She came to stand beside him in the almost dark. They stood there in silence for a few minutes, just looking at the twinkling lights on the tree.

"It's beautiful, isn't it?" she whispered, sounding almost reverent.

Though it lacked the expensive elegance of the Christmas trees various housekeepers had erected during his childhood, it was the prettiest tree he'd ever seen. Being a part of this moment with this small family filled him with a contentment and a sense of belonging he hadn't known he'd been missing.

"All it needs to be complete is some presents under it—" she looked at Shawn "—but we have to wait for Santa Claus to bring those, don't we?"

"Santa Claus," the boy repeated in awe, and looked at Paxton.

He and Lauren laughed.

"Who's hungry?" she asked.

"I would be guilty of that." Paxton raised his hand.

"Give me a few minutes and I'll have supper on the table." Lauren headed toward the kitchen with her son on her hip.

Paxton followed. "What can I do to help?"

She slipped Shawn into a highchair. "You can get the dishes and drinks together."

Over the next few minutes they worked side by side, setting their places, making a salad and putting the casserole on the table. Paxton finished by pouring the drinks.

Lauren finished a bite of food. "I thought you'd be messing around in your lab all night."

"I missed my new friend." He gave her a look meant to convey an underlying meaning.

"You did?"

"I did." His gaze held hers.

A few minutes later he looked at Lauren to find her watching him thoughtfully, tapping her fork against her bottom lip. The one he longed to kiss. "Okay, what's going on in that mind of yours?"

"I was just thinking you know a lot more about me than I do about you."

He didn't like where this was headed. "There's not much to tell that you don't already know."

"I don't believe that." She pursed her lips and watched him.

Paxton lowered his chin and gave her a narrow-eyed look in an effort to intimidate her into not pushing him for information. "I thought you looked me up on the internet."

"I did, but I'd like to hear the whole story from you. I don't want to read what others have to say."

Paxton pushed back his chair, the legs scraping the floor, but he didn't stand. It was time to face what had happened and telling Lauren would be his first step to doing so. If he had to confide in someone, she was a good choice. Even if she saw him as a pity case.

He started off slowly. "I guess I'm like most of the people in my family over the last four generations—I'm a physician. But you already know that. I love being a doctor. Have always wanted to be one. But I think that's where it ends."

"Where what ends?" She shifted so she could see him better.

"Our similarities. My grandfather and his brothers started a clinic, later a hospital that made the name Samuels mean something in Boston society. With that came the constant pressure to meet the 'obligations' attached to the family name as I grew up. I never understood that. I was an outsider from the beginning, I think. It never occurred to my parents that I might want to do something different with my life other than be a Boston Samuels. You should have seen the brawl it brought on when I informed my parents I was going to the Peace Corps. You would have thought I had asked them all to join. I feared my mother might never recover." He smiled ironically.

"But you went anyway." She sounded proud of him for doing that.

His ego had been stroked. "I did, but I had already signed all the papers and there wasn't much they could do about it then. Kind of like me coming out here…"

"They should have been happy when you returned from the Peace Corps, though, right?"

"Oh, they were, but nothing had changed. If anything, they wanted me to do more, be more. I thought I might feel different after being away, that they might have seen a difference in me and understood what I wanted."

"So when a chance to do something different came around, like coming out here, you jumped at it."

"Something like that. It was more like I needed to get out of Boston, and this was a way to escape."

"Why?"

Now they were back to the wedding business. He had no choice but to admit what had happened. "I was engaged. My family and hers had been friends forever. We'd been together since childhood. It just seemed the natural progression for us to get married. I don't know why I went along with it. I guess I was too busy trying to make my parents happy that I got caught up in the idea."

"So what happened?"

If he told it really fast, maybe it wouldn't hurt so much, or the humiliation be so great. "Two weeks before our wedding, I was shown explicit pictures of

Gabriella and another man posted all over the internet. Turns out she was cheating on me."

Lauren's hiss of shock filled the air. "I'm sorry, Paxton. That is wrong on so many levels."

She was right.

"I shouldn't have pushed you to talk about it."

"It's okay. It felt good to get it out." Truthfully, it did.

Lauren put her hand over his, which was now lying on the table. "You do know that her infidelity was about her poor character and not about who you are. You're a fine man, Paxton Samuels. An excellent doctor and you have a good heart. She messed up big time in losing you."

Coming from Lauren, he found he was starting to believe it. "Along with the embarrassment that something like that had happened to me was the betrayal of my parents encouraging me to forgive her and let the wedding go on. I refused, saw this job posting and came out here to let the story die down."

"My husband ran around on me, too," she said quietly, then looked startled. "I've never told anyone that before. I guess I just didn't want you to think you were alone."

Bile rose in his throat. He was disgusted with himself. Here he was feeling sorry for himself and she'd experienced the same thing. "Do you mind telling me about it?"

She shrugged. "There's not much to tell. He came to town with the oil company. I fell hard. I'd been looking for a way to get out of town and see the world. Mark was the answer. We married then proceeded to live in five towns in a year. He was cheating on me in all of them. I told him I was pregnant the day he died in an oil-rig explosion. I came back here and rebuilt my life. I'm planning to give Shawn a good life here."

"I guess we have more in common than we thought."

She gave him a wry smile. "I guess we do. Not necessarily good stuff, but stuff."

Paxton chuckled. "You have a point there."

Shawn dropped his truck to the floor, and without thinking Paxton handed it back to him with a smile. Maybe he was getting used to this game after all.

"It's time for me to give Shawn a bath and put him to bed." Lauren stood and lifted Shawn from his chair.

Paxton stood as well. "I guess that's your nice way of saying it's time for me to go."

"That's not what I meant at all. I just wanted you to know that things will be pretty busy around here until I get Shawn to sleep."

"It's okay. I've intruded on your family time long enough. I have a couple of things I need to do in the lab anyway."

Lauren walked him to the front door. "I didn't intend to run you off."

Paxton was relieved by the convenient excuse to get going. The more he was around Lauren and Shawn the more involved he became in their lives. He didn't plan to stay in Last Stop much longer and he was confident he wasn't the man to give Lauren what she wanted or needed. She planned to stay here and he had obligations in Boston. It was his home. Just like Last Stop was Lauren's. They shared some past hurts but their futures were down different paths.

Yet there was an emotional pull between them. He couldn't help it—he leaned in for a kiss.

She pulled back, waving her hand between them. "Paxton, I don't know if that's such a good idea. You're leaving. I'm staying. You've recently been hurt. I fell for a guy who was just passing through, and look how that worked out. I think we should be careful here."

"You're probably right but I'm attracted to you. I believe you are to me. There doesn't have to be any strings attached. We could be just two people enjoying each other."

In spite of the fact he saw no future for them either, he felt a gut-wrenching desire to make love to her.

"I don't know about where you come from, but a kiss like the one we shared means something. I have Shawn to think about, and my reputation as well. You'll be gone and I'll still be here."

He met her serious gaze. "That kiss meant something to me as well. We're both adults so why can't we enjoy this while we can?"

Why did it matter so much that she agree to a brief affair? Maybe because he already knew that he wouldn't get his fill of her in a one-night stand.

She studied him a moment before her hand came around his neck and she nudged him closer. Coming up on her toes she gave him an open-mouthed kiss. Heat blazed through him. Just as quickly, she backed away and opened the door.

In a daze he walked out of the house. The cold night air was in direct contrast to the hot flow of his blood.

CHAPTER SEVEN

LAUREN COULDN'T BELIEVE she'd kissed Paxton like that. Over the next two days, she'd expected him to try to kiss her back. She'd already tossed out caution like old clothes—she wanted him to kiss her with every fiber of her being. Despite jitters of anticipation keeping her alert to Paxton's every move and word, it didn't happen. He remained professional the entire time, much to her disappointment, despite her warning that it should be that way between them. If his goal was to have her on edge, he had achieved it.

It had been years since she'd last felt that distinct feminine yearning for a man simmering below the surface. The zip that made her feel vibrantly alive. Being a mother was fulfilling but there was nothing like being desired by a man. Paxton had made it clear he wanted her and yet...

Their highly personal conversation had moved their relationship to a new level. In a sad way they had bonded over a terrible time in each of their lives. As different as their outside worlds were, their private ones had been a lot alike.

On Friday evening, she left for the day without any indication from him that he might turn up for dinner

or that she would see him over the weekend. With reluctance, she gave up hope on any further intimacy
between them. It was better that way. There was no
chance for hurt on either side. They'd both had enough
of that. Already she'd let Paxton Samuels matter far
more than he should.

It was Christmastime and the community dinner
and dance was tomorrow evening. She planned to concentrate on having a good time without him.

With her resolution made, she dressed for the event
on Saturday, pushing Paxton out of her thoughts.
Shawn looked so cute in his new outfit. She'd enjoyed putting on her red dress and knowing her appearance was at its best. The annual event was her
favorite one of the year.

The community center had never looked more festive. The ladies in town had outdone themselves, decorating. A large tree stood in the corner with colorful
bright lights adorning its boughs. Beneath were presents of all shapes and sizes for the smaller children.
Lauren pointed them out to her wide-eyed son, who
was holding on to her hand as though she might vanish.

The tables were draped with dark green cloths with
red runners going down the center. Candles flickered
in tall holders positioned at regular intervals. Napkins
and silverware dressed each dining space.

Long tables had been pushed together and covered
with matching green cloths to form the buffet table.
They were so heavy with food Lauren imagined they
almost groaned beneath their burden. She grinned. It
was an unwritten rule that there was competition between the women over who had brought the best dish.

Everybody was dressed in their holiday finery. A small dance floor had been set up in the center of the room with an even smaller stage nearby. The overhead lights were dimmed so that miniature lights hanging from every imaginable spot on the ceiling and walls shone brilliantly.

Lauren's attention was drawn to the entrance. Her heart beat faster. *Paxton.* What had made him decide to come? Heat filled her cheeks. It didn't matter. She was glad to see him. He looked handsome in a dark suit accented by a red tie.

He strolled toward her as if they had planned this. She said with schooled politeness, "Hello. I didn't expect to see you."

With a nonchalant shrug, he offered, "I enjoyed the parade so much I thought I might like this too." He openly considered her for a moment, as if his eyes couldn't leave her. Speaking reverently, he said, "You look amazing."

She had no doubt her cheeks matched the color of her dress. The compliment shot straight to her heart. She'd taken care with her hair by pulling it back and up, leaving some tendrils loosely curling around her face. Her dress fit her to perfection, emphasizing her figure in all the right ways, but it wasn't until Paxton had voiced his appreciation that she believed she might look exceptional. His compliment she would treasure long after he'd left Last Stop.

"Thank you." Paxton brought out an uncharacteristic bashfulness in her. "You look nice also. I like that reindeer tie. Is it new?"

"It's a little something I picked up the other day

when I was shopping." He grinned at her. "Festive, isn't it?"

"For a man who isn't into Christmas, that sure screams it."

He held her gaze. "Maybe I've changed my mind."

Was he talking about the tie or her? Whichever it was, she was still glad to see him.

Their attention was drawn to the stage by the mayor announcing into the microphone, "I'm not going to make a speech." A cheer went up. "But I do want to say how nice everything looks, especially the food, and say thank you to everyone who worked so hard on this evening. Also, I want to remind everyone to have their picture taken at the photo booth tonight. We want everyone's picture for the history book Mrs. Elise is putting together. Now, Reverend Bishop, will you bless our food? Oh, and Merry Christmas, everyone."

The reverend was brief, and within five minutes everyone either stood on both sides of the buffet tables, filling their plates, or were in line with plates at the ready.

"Let me have Shawn while you fill your plates. I'll come back for mine," Paxton suggested.

Lauren looked at him. She'd not really minded him not being too comfortable around her son, because the last thing she needed was for her child to become attached to a man who wouldn't be around long. But this did feel nice...

"We'll manage. You keep your place in line. Those dishes are emptying fast." Lauren didn't want him to feel like he had to take care of them.

"Don't argue. By the time I come back the line

won't be that long and I seriously doubt the matrons of this town will let me go hungry."

"Thanks. I would appreciate the help." It was nice to have the assistance. Who was she kidding? Having Paxton around was wonderful. She liked the attention, the feel of walking a little straighter because she was on the arm of a handsome man.

With two plates full to the brim, Lauren looked for Paxton in the large room.

"He's over there by the tree, honey," one of the older women said. "It looks like Shawn has taken a liking to him."

Lauren just smiled. She'd found them. Paxton was showing an ornament to Shawn. Their heads were together and Paxton was listening to something Shawn was babbling. Lauren's heart caught. Did she dare hope for...?

She and Shawn had survived Mark's death to become a happy little family. Having her mother and father close, as well as her brothers, had been helpful, but something was missing. Shawn needed a father and she needed...to be needed as a woman. To give and receive what a man and woman could give each other. With Paxton, could that be possible? Would he stay and let that happen? Had he even considered it?

His face brightened when he saw her and he said something to Shawn. They came toward her. Paxton reached for one of the plates and carefully placed it on the table. Lauren put the other down.

"I'll get a highchair. I saw one over in the corner. Be right back." He was gone before she could object.

"Hey, I've been trying to get your attention," a woman said behind them.

Lauren turned. "Hi, Mom."

"I was saving you a place until I couldn't anymore, but I see you have a good one here." She looked off in Paxton's direction and smiled.

"Don't start getting any ideas, Mom."

"I didn't say anything, but it's nice to see you smile for a change."

"Hey, Mrs. Tucker. How're you?" Paxton asked after placing the highchair at the end of the table.

"Hi, Dr. Samuels," her mother responded in a welcoming manner.

"Paxton, please."

Her mother smiled. "Are you enjoying yourself?"

"I am. The parade was great so I thought I'd give this a try." He took Shawn and slipped him into the highchair like a pro. This was different. If Paxton was warming up to Shawn to get to her, it was working.

"My, you're good at that." Her mother gave her a meaningful look.

That earned her mother a warning smile. "Mom, your food's getting cold. I know ours is. We'll see you later on."

When her mother was beyond earshot, Lauren looked at Paxton. "Sorry about that. Mom means well but she can be pushy."

Paxton chuckled. "She doesn't even get in the game with my mother."

Shawn squealed his impatience and Lauren sighed. "Okay, honey. I know you're ready to eat."

They all settled in for the meal. Soon the table had filled all around them, everyone talking and laughing.

This event was nothing like the sedate and proper occasions Paxton had attended all his life. Boisterous laughter was coming from different areas in the building. Everyone here was truly enjoying each other's company, and the season. These folks weren't going through the motions of socializing in a bored haze or checking the time to see how soon they could slip away without being rude. He should have felt out of place but instead he felt at home.

Lauren wiped some food off Shawn's face and said, "Sweetpea, we need to go speak to Nannie and PaPa."

"Who?" Paxton asked.

"My parents."

Lauren started pulling Shawn out of the highchair. His legs didn't come out smoothly. Paxton quickly took over. "Let me give it a try." Seconds later he had Shawn out and in his arms.

One of the ladies sitting nearby said, "You're a natural at that."

He grinned, filling up with pride. "Thanks."

"I'll take him," Lauren offered, a tad too quickly for his liking.

Did she have a problem with him becoming friendly with Shawn? Maybe he had been a little unsure around Shawn but the boy was starting to grow on him. "I'd like to go with you and meet your father."

Lauren gave him a skeptical look. "Okay, but remember whatever happens this was your idea." They weaved through the crowd toward the other side of the building.

As they passed the photo area setup Lauren said, "I'm going to get this over with now when there's no line." She spoke to the ultra-thin man standing nearby. "Mr. John, Shawn and I are ready, if you are?"

"Sure. Come sit right here." Mr. John placed a stool

in front of a backdrop scene of a tree with its branches laden with snow, a blanket of white all around and a rabbit looking out from behind a smaller tree.

Lauren took a seat, holding Shawn in her lap. He squirmed but soon stilled. The photographer stepped away. She looked at him and smiled. Shawn followed her lead.

The photographer said, "Raise your chin, just a little. That's it." Click, click. "Wonderful." He looked back at Paxton. "Why don't you get in it? The mayor wants one of everybody."

"But we aren't…" Lauren left it hanging.

Together, Paxton finished in silence. They weren't a couple. A family. All together. But what would it really matter for a few pictures? The picture would only be seen by a few in a small-town history book that no one would ever be interested in.

Lauren shook her head in a rueful manner before motioning to him. "Aw, come on."

Paxton jogged the few steps over to join them.

"I want you to stand behind Lauren, young man. Place your hand on her shoulder. Now, all I need you to do is smile." There were a couple of clicks. "We're going to need to try that again. Shawn turned before I had it. Dr. Samuels, take Shawn," the photographer instructed.

Paxton and Lauren looked at each other a moment before she handed Shawn to him.

"Lauren, just stay put," Mr. John said. He stepped away then brought another stool close.

"Doctor, sit on the stool and spread your legs wide and scoot up close to Lauren. Now, Lauren, turn your legs this direction." Mr. John adjusted them.

Paxton relished the warmth of Lauren against him as she obeyed.

"Hang on, buddy. This shouldn't take long." Paxton grinned at Shawn and made him giggle. Lauren was close enough that his breath caused her hair to move. Had she shivered?

"Now, that looks good." The photographer started clicking the camera with zeal.

Lauren glanced back. Her gaze met his. Could she see the desire in his eyes?

She blinked and gave him a soft smile.

"That got it. Thanks," Mr. John said, breaking the moment.

Lauren didn't move, neither did he.

There were a few snickers around them.

A line had formed while they were having their picture taken. From the cozy position they were in and with him holding Shawn, they must have looked like a happy family. One that he would never really be a part of even if he wanted to, which he didn't. Stepping out of one difficult relationship into another between two people who obviously wanted different things in life would never work. His duties were hundreds of miles away from Last Stop. Paxton moved back and Lauren stood quickly, grabbed her son and walked away.

"Hey, wait," Paxton said behind her.

She didn't slow as he followed her. She hurried through and around small cheerful groups as if she were running from him. Finally she stopped at a table where the people were still eating and listening to a large man who was telling a story.

Lauren placed her hand on her mother's shoulder. Paxton stood beside Lauren. Her mother covered it with her own. She leaned toward Lauren and said in a loud whisper, "It'll be a few minutes. Your dad's stories can be long."

Paxton nodded. So the over-large man with the deep voice was Lauren's father. After seeing him, Paxton thought better of wanting to meet him. He looked intimidating. The thought that Mr. Gerhart might be a marshmallow compared to Lauren's father had been completely correct.

With most of the women Paxton dated, he'd known their fathers most of his life. He'd felt some trepidation at being around those men, but he had at least had the confidence of being a member of Boston's newest generation of socialites. In Last Stop he was an outsider, and a temporary one at that. Worse, he had a sense that fathers around this area took protecting what was theirs in a very literal, basic sense, particularly their daughters.

A few minutes later the story ended with people around them laughing. When everyone had quietened, Lauren's father turned to look at him.

"Hey, Dad," Lauren said. "I wanted to say hi and introduce you to Dr. Samuels."

"Paxton, sir." Paxton extended his hand.

Mr. Tucker accepted it and looked Paxton straight in the eyes. The man's steady stare warned him. *Don't hurt my daughter.*

Paxton let go of the elder man's strong grip. He couldn't promise that. There wasn't enough clarity about his own life to promise anything to anyone else. While they stood there Shawn reached his arms out to Paxton. He took the boy from a reluctant-looking Lauren.

"I see that you and my grandson have become friends," her father offered in an affable tone.

"Yeah, I guess we have." Paxton looked at Lauren then at Shawn. He was starting to care for them far more than he was ready to admit.

The five-person band started playing a slow Christmas carol and a few couples moved toward the dance floor.

"Why don't you give me Shawn and you and Lauren go have a dance?" Mrs. Tucker suggested with a twinkle in her dark eyes, so like her daughter's.

"Mom!" Lauren exclaimed, embarrassment darkening her face.

Paxton gave her a pointed look. "You don't think I know how to dance?"

"I wasn't saying that. I'm sure you're a fine dancer," Lauren declared with a glare, her voice higher than usual.

"Come see Nannie." Mrs. Tucker reached for the boy.

Paxton released Shawn to his grandmother and took hold of Lauren's clenched hand before she could protest further, leading her through the crowd to the dance floor. With an experienced twirl, Paxton brought her into his arms. She came willingly and fit perfectly. He led her in the two-step around the open area. Lauren followed effortlessly, and breathlessly.

Her dress swirled around his legs as he moved her backward then pulled her to him. When that dance was over he didn't stop and instead they moved into the next one. Paxton seamlessly led her into a quickstep. He held her tight as he shifted her without a misstep. Lauren followed his lead with grace and con-

134 A DADDY SENT BY SANTA

fidence. Their partnership seemed perfect. Would it be the same elsewhere? Like in bed?

He looked into her eyes. They were watching him, smiling. That protective look he'd seen earlier had disappeared. "You're an amazing dancer."

"Thanks. Required lessons in my world. No *F*s allowed."

"That bad?"

"Only if you'd rather be outside, catching frogs in the pond."

She giggled. A lovely sound that could only be hers. "I can see your point."

"My mother didn't when the housekeeper couldn't get the stain out of my shirt."

"Well, whatever your hardship was, it's my enjoyment now. This is the most fun I've had in a long time."

"Then let me show you a couple of moves I keep hidden for special occasions." Paxton grinned then pushed her away and brought her back to him before turning her and tipping her back in a dip.

Lauren laughed deeply. The sound flowed through him like a warm drink that could thaw and dilute all the ugliness he'd brought with him to Last Stop. He pulled her to him and they started off again.

"I can't remember the last time I had so much fun," she said, her voice full of happiness. "If I could bottle this moment and keep it forever, I would."

Had another woman ever made him feel like the most special man on earth? Lauren's praise had that power.

The band went into another fast number and they separated except for Paxton's hold on one of her hands.

It was clear to Lauren that they were a well-paired couple on the dance floor, and apparently it was just as evident to everyone else because none of her male friends tried to cut in. After that the band took a break and they found their way back to her parents and Shawn.

"Paxton, you've made a mistake," Lauren's mother greeted him.

"What have I done?" He looked around him.

"You're going to have to dance with every woman in town or give the men dancing lessons!"

Everyone around them erupted in laughter.

"I wouldn't mind having one of those dances," a woman of about eighty called.

"Maybe next time. I saved my arsenal of dances for someone special tonight." The look he gave Lauren made it clear he meant her. After being in his arms, she wanted more. If he could dance so magnificently she could only imagine Paxton's skills at making love.

She gave him a shy smile. "It's time I got Shawn home to bed."

"Your dad, Shawn and I have been talking," her mother said, blocking her effort to take her son from his grandfather's arms. "And Shawn decided he wanted to spend the night with us. We could bring him home around bedtime tomorrow evening. That way you two could dance some more. You looked like you were enjoying yourselves."

Lauren felt as if she'd walked into a trap. She'd been in Paxton's arms, had been his partner. The one he'd chosen. But in a couple of weeks he'd be back in Boston, choosing some other woman to dance with. She couldn't let this go further. "But, Mom, that's too much—"

Her mother said, for her ears only, "Honey, you need to enjoy yourself while you can. You haven't in so long. Shawn deserves a happy mother."

She couldn't argue with that logic even if she wanted to. Her mother only wanted her to continue having fun, which she most definitely had been having in Paxton's strong arms.

"Okay, if that's what y'all have cooked up. 'Night, sweetpea." Lauren kissed Shawn. "See you tomorrow."

"Goodnight, Shawn." Paxton ran the back of his finger over Shawn's cheek.

Lauren's chest tightened as those what-if questions started flowing through her mind again. She accompanied her parents to where their coats hung, helped her mother bundle Shawn up and then watched her walk away with him. Moments later she turned and discovered Paxton standing behind her.

"I take it that Shawn doesn't sleep over often." Paxton watched her with thoughtful eyes.

"No. Well, he has more in the last couple of weeks than he has his entire life."

"So that night in the hotel was the first?"

She nodded.

"That's why you kept calling him all the time."

Lauren looked at him with surprise. "I was that obvious?"

"Actually, no, but I might have been less jealous if I had known the whole situation."

"Jealous?"

Paxton grinned. "How was I supposed to know he was your son? Come on, let's dance some more before you have me embarrassing myself further."

She hesitated then took his hand. His grip was warm and strong, yet gentle. It was only dancing, she told herself. That pleasure was publicly acceptable and didn't imply they were anything more than friends. With that consolation in mind she allowed him to escort her back to the floor. They continued to dance until the number of partying people thinned.

During the last song Paxton held her close. There was comforting security in his arms. She longed for that haven. Last Stop had provided that for her and Shawn when she'd returned, but she needed human sanctuary as well. Would she be willing to leave Last Stop if Paxton asked her to? No. She couldn't take that chance again. Whatever was happening between them now, she had to enjoy it for what it was—a passing fling. Shawn needed what Last Stop could give him. What he had around him now. The loving care of a close-knit community.

"Hey," Paxton breathed into her ear. "We'd better go. They're closing up the show."

She looked around. Men were stacking chairs. "I should help."

"I bet that you do that every time there's an event."

Lauren gave him a sheepish look. "Most of them."

"Then I'd guess they could survive one without you. Let's go look at the stars."

Her heart jumped. How long had it been since she'd look at the stars with a man? Too long. "Okay."

They pulled their cold-weather clothing on and stepped out into the chilly but clear night.

Paxton held her hand as they strolled along the road toward her house. Without saying anything, she led him around to the back of the house to where they could see over the plain for miles. There were occasional homes with lights on to mar the view but otherwise the stars were big and bright. They took a seat on the picnic table near Shawn's swing set.

Paxton placed his arm around her shoulders and pulled her close. She laid her head into the curve of his shoulder. It was perfect. "You don't get this in the city."

He kissed the top of her head. "There're a lot of things you do here that I don't get in the city. Nice things. Peaceful pleasures."

"Such as?"

"Now you're stalling for time, I think. You know you have to make a decision here, don't you, Lauren?"

"I thought I might," she whispered, unsure what to say. She knew what she wanted, but would it be the right thing in the long run, or would it bring on hurt? But why should it? They could have a nice time together then it would all be over when he left. If they both understood that going in, then all would be fine.

"I'd like to stay the night." Paxton was watching her.

His breath formed small clouds in the cold air. Would it change things if she agreed? Or didn't? The only thing she knew for sure was that she wanted this time with Paxton, even if it was short. From it she would have enough satisfying memories to last the rest of her life.

Lauren stood and reached out her hand, "Come on, you must be getting cold."

CHAPTER EIGHT

PAXTON FOLLOWED HER up the back steps and through the door into her kitchen. A single light from the living room illuminated what little he could see. Unable to ignore his desire, he pulled Lauren into his arms. His heart throbbed against his chest as she came willingly. Even through her outer clothing he could feel her curves. Ones he sought to caress.

Her arms came up around his shoulders, her hands along the sides of his face until she'd pushed his knit cap off. His lips found her cool ones. He wanted more, so much more. She offered him entrance, which he gladly accepted, anticipating the heat to come. Her tongue met his and they danced, sending his passion soaring.

Lauren's hands tugged at his gloves, removing them. Seconds later her attention centered on the top button of his coat, releasing it. She went down to the next and down again, continuing until she could shove his coat open and step inside to wrap her arms around his waist. She wiggled against him. "It feels so good here."

Paxton felt his body hardening. He pulled her tight. "I know other ways to make you feel good."

She stepped back, forcing him to relax his hold, and studied him for a minute. Was she trying to decide whether or not to let him stay? Hadn't she already agreed or was that just him wanting the night so desperately he was reading more into her actions and words than she intended?

By the time Lauren took his hand it shook. She led him to her bedroom. He had his answer. When she didn't turn on a light, he flipped on the lamp beside the bed. "I want to see you, as well as enjoy you. I don't want anything between us, not even the darkness."

Her eyes glistened with emotion. She started removing her coat. Paxton placed his hand on hers. "I'd like that."

She nodded.

He took her hat off. There was a deep roll of humor in his throat as he fought the static electricity making her hair stand out around her head. Tenderly he ran his hands over it, smoothing it into place. "I love your hair. It's like a mass of wild silk."

Running a hand down the sleeve of her coat to her hand, he lifted it and slowly pulled off her glove one finger at a time. He did the same for the other, letting both fall to the floor.

Never breaking eye contact, she unwrapped his scarf and pulled it away from his neck, letting it slip through her fingers to pool at her feet. Using both hands, Lauren pushed his coat from his shoulders. It hit the floor with a soft thud. He met her heated gaze. Had she registered a dare in his eyes?

He hoped so. Cupping her beautiful face in his hands, he kissed her with all the fervor throbbing through him. Her responsiveness let him know she was as eager to spend time with him as he was with her. His ego and self-esteem, so thoroughly damaged by Gabriella's rejection, was rapidly healing from Lauren's ministrations.

He'd have never believed he would be able to trust again. In a few short weeks Lauren had healed his damaged ego. Helping him find the joy in life he'd been searching for with such desperation. Having lived encircled by family, he had thought well-being would come naturally, but the older he got the more aware he'd become of its absence.

During their kiss he finished removing her outer clothing. Holding himself in check was becoming more difficult. He wanted Lauren now. To feel all of her surrounding him. Holding him. Loving him.

"Please sit on the bed." When she hesitated, he kissed her neck. Her tell-tale shiver gratified his masculinity.

After she was seated, he lifted her foot and removed her red high-heeled shoe. Tossing it beside their clothes, he went after the other. It landed close to its mate. Placing her foot on his thigh, he slowly ran his hand over her calf, then beneath her knee and up under her dress. Paxton's hand abruptly stopped. His breathing jumped way up the scale.

Was that what he thought it was?

He looked at Lauren. In a teasing tone he said, "Now, what do we have here?"

A mysterious smile came to her lips. "My garter belt."

With a hard thump of his heart against his chest, he felt himself go rock hard. No woman, to his knowledge, wore a garter belt. Tight jeans and boots to black hose and garter belt, Lauren was the best of contradictions. Surprise and soft seduction. What other sweet surprises was she hiding? He wanted to find out.

His fingers paused over the belt snap. Like a knight requesting a favor from his queen, he asked, "May I?"

"No."

What? He might die if he didn't. "No?"

He raised his eyebrows. She held his world in her answer.

She grinned. "Just unsnap it, would you?"

"That I can do." Despite his inexperience, he flipped the snap and then the other. His hands shook as he slowly brushed the silky stocking down her leg; he kissed the top of her foot before placing it on the floor. "Yum, that was so nice, I think I'll do it again."

He was rewarded with that giggle he loved so much. A few minutes later her other shapely leg was bare. If he didn't have her soon his self-control would fail and he'd be humiliated. Standing, he offered his hands and she placed hers in his, allowing him to help her to her feet.

Lauren's hands flattened over his chest. She slid them up until she reached his tie. Untying it, she pulled it from around his neck in a tantalizingly slow movement. Her lips found his as she pushed his suit jacket. It fell on the growing pile of clothing with a hushed thud. When Paxton reached to take her she blocked his hands with unmistakable firmness and returned to unbuttoning his shirt down to his pants. When she went for the fastener of those he stopped her.

"Oh, no." He gently clasped her hands. "It's my turn

now." His hands lightly rested on her waist and rotated her until her back faced him. Taking the pull of the metal zipper, he gently tugged downward. He placed a kiss on the exposed skin just below her neck, feeling her quiver as he opened the dress. Against her skin he breathed, "I've never seen someone look lovelier or sexier in a dress. And red. I don't know which was hotter, you or the dress."

She turned, taking his face in her small soft hands and kissing him. Instead of the sweet kiss of thanks he was expecting, this one made his blood thunder in his veins and he felt his desire rise. Her arms slipped around his neck as she opened wide to greet him with her tongue. She teased and taunted, increasing the heat from simmering to boiling.

Paxton walked her back against the bed.

"Not yet." She stopped him with a hand to his chest. "Still too many clothes."

He grinned. "I can take care of that." He reached for her.

"Not mine. Yours." She grasped his undershirt, leisurely pulling it up, then planting kisses over his heart and nibbling her way up to his chin. His discomfort shot up a couple of more notches. When she finally loosened his pants, he stepped away and kicked off his shoes, letting his clothing drop to the floor. Stepping out of the puddle of his pants, Paxton peeled off his socks with impatience and made a purposeful move toward Lauren.

In a low, teasing growl he declared, "No more playing."

It felt so good to have fun with a woman. To enjoy the moment and not think about what was next on the agenda. He'd been going through the motions of sex by "appointment" with his former fiancée for so long he'd forgotten the erotic bliss of truly desiring a woman.

Lauren turned but he caught her. She laughed when he announced, "As much as I love that red dress, it has to go."

She stood still before him as he pushed the silken fabric down her arms. The material swished as it flowed around her until it settled on the floor. Lauren was now clad in only a red skimpy bra, matching panties and a black lace garter belt.

Her beauty took his breath. "Heaven help me, Lauren, I'm glad I didn't know what you were wearing or I would've embarrassed us both."

She grew solemn and lowered her eyes, as if unsure of the compliment.

"Hey, look at me." She did. "You're the sexiest woman I've ever seen."

A shy smile covered her kiss-swollen lips.

"There's only one thing wrong." Her mouth dropped a fraction. "I'd rather see you in nothing." He lifted her and fell back onto the bed. "And I intend to," he growled close to her ear. His hand went to her narrow waist. Despite having had a child, she still had a slim figure. Her skin was as smooth as he had imagined. Perfect. Paxton followed the curve up until the pad of his thumb rested beneath one of her breasts.

The hitch in her breathing when he cupped her was gratifying. Even through the lace Paxton could feel her hard nipple erect against his palm. As he gave her a tender kiss, his hand moved around to unclip her bra. Unable to wait any longer, he pushed it up and filled both hands with the rich firmness of her breasts.

She sighed.

Paxton held one high then placed a kiss on the nipple before taking the tip between his lips. He sucked as Lauren's fingers funneled through his hair then traveled to gently knead his back, as though begging for more. Paxton shifted his devotion to her other breast, giving it equal attention.

Sometime later, as he showered her face, shoulders and neck with tender kisses, he removed the bra completely and let it slip from his fingers. Laying her back upon the bed, his hands explored all that she offered until one finger followed the tiny line of elastic low on her hips.

"You're such an amazing package of surprises." He admired her spread out on the bed just for him. "All tough looking on the outside and all sexy matching lace on the inside. Who would have thought?"

Her eyelids lowered, giving her a sensual come-hither look. "Have you been thinking about me?"

"Hell, yeah," he growled. "Why do you think I've spent so much time in the damn lab?"

"Just what've you been thinking?" she asked with a naughty note as she ran a finger down his arm.

"That I'd like to see you like this. Lying on the bed just for me. The moonlight highlighting your assets, all the ones I want to caress, plan to caress."

Lauren kissed two of her fingers and placed them on his mouth before she trailed her hand down over his chest. His manhood jumped in anticipation. He had to have Lauren soon. But she deserved better than a raging bull mounting her.

Her hand almost slipped beneath his underwear before he grabbed it. Once she touched him his self-control would fail. He leaned over and kissed her, directing her thoughts elsewhere. His hand flattened on her perfect belly. Lauren hissed under her breath. Paxton loved her reactions to his touch.

Using his forefinger, he traced the line of her panties and slipped all four fingers beneath to brush her curls. Lauren squirmed and parted her legs. That was the invitation he'd been hoping for. He gave her panties a tug, and with the lift of her hips they were gone.

Paxton's gaze met hers as he outlined her belly button. Her eyes widened, then slowly lowered to a reflective level as his forefinger slid between her thighs. Capturing her lips with his mouth before his finger entered her wet, hot passage. When it did, she jerked forward, her body tightening in welcoming acceptance. Paxton removed his finger, then slid it back in, using a rhythmic manner attuned to the thrusts of his tongue. He increased the speed. Lauren whimpered, then groaned and thrashed, her hips lifting to meet his actions. With each reaction his need grew, but her pleasure remained his focus.

With a final push that matched the ultimate invasion of his tongue, he took her over the edge. Rising up, he watched her reaction. Lauren's eyes squeezed closed then opened wide in surprise, meeting his as she flew off into bliss. Could anything be more stunning?

He'd never done that before. Sex had always been something he enjoyed but he hadn't reached the level of ecstasy he'd found with Lauren. For once in his life, perhaps for the first time, he was giving all of himself.

Lauren returned to reality to see Paxton standing and searching his pants pocket. He soon sheathed himself and joined her again.

"You're the most amazing woman I know. I can't wait…"

His passionate expression, green eyes aglow with sincerity, told her he meant every word. When had a man said something that sweet to her?

Who Paxton was, his sheer magnitude, tugged at her. Her attraction had steadily grown stronger since the night they'd first met. Each movement he made while they worked together registered in her awareness with uncommon intensity. What he might be doing on their days off had been a constant distraction to her own plans.

With Mark, lovemaking had been frenzied with lust and over almost before it began, with little time to feel. Paxton had yet to do anything significant and she was feeling too much. But that would change now. Arms wide, she welcomed him.

Without hesitation he slipped inside her. His length and bulk caught her by surprise for a second. But when he started the familiar yet unique movement that she recognized as theirs alone, she came alive. Her legs went around his waist. As Paxton moved inside her, Lauren's heels pulled him closer. He pushed her higher, applying pressure. She had been out of control before but this time as she spiraled upward toward that peak of sweet release, the journey was honeyed, oh, so sweet. Beyond anything she'd experienced or even imagined before.

Thrusting harder and faster until he caught up with her at the very edge of endurance, they joined each

other in oblivion. After an almost endless perfect moment they settled, each breathing hard. Paxton pulled
a blanket from the foot of the bed over them and rolled
to spoon Lauren into his body. She'd never felt so se-
cure in her life.

Sometime before daybreak, Lauren woke. For a second she was startled. There was a man in her bed.
She'd been sleeping alone for nearly three years now
and had almost forgotten… Yet Paxton was so unlike her memories of Mark. With Paxton her emotions were deeper, more sensual, heightened. She was
more aware of every nuance of sensation. When he
was gone she would miss the miraculous transforma-
tion from just existing to being vitally alive.

She wasn't kidding herself. Paxton would leave
town. He had responsibilities elsewhere. He might be
working on his lab as if he intended to stay yet he'd
never indicated in word or deed that he was.

But that didn't matter right now. She needed this,
him, their temporary union, to awaken her dormant
femininity. She'd been suppressing her womanhood
in an almost superhuman effort to be both mother and
father to her son. This was for her.

"Hey," Paxton said in that clipped accent she knew
so well.

She rolled to face him. "Hey, yourself."

"What're you thinking about over there?"

"How do you know I was thinking anything?" Was
she really that predictable?

"I don't know…because maybe I've gotten to know
you pretty well. I've worked with you for a couple of
weeks. I've spent evenings, now the night with you.

I've watched you with Shawn and the people who live in Last Stop."

He really got her. She wanted someone in her life like that. Who was she kidding? She wanted him. Would he ever consider making Last Stop his home? "You know we have a need for a good doctor here. No strings attached, I promised."

He quickly had her on her back. "Aw, but the strings would be the selling point." Paxton's lips found hers. A few moments later as his mouth moved along her neck and he cupped her breast he murmured, "Along with a few other perks."

Lauren giggled. This she could get used to. Did she dare get her hopes up that this time would be different?

The next evening when Paxton left Lauren's house he'd never felt happier, freer. It was becoming increasingly clear that he was getting attached to Lauren, even Shawn—but that couldn't continue. He would be leaving soon and it wasn't fair to any of them, yet he couldn't stay away. The more time he spent with them the more difficult it would be for him to return to Boston. If things were different with his father would he, could he stay in Last Stop?

If he could have come up with a good excuse, he would have returned to her house later, but he figured if she wanted him there she would have called him. She probably wanted to spend time with Shawn. Couldn't she do that with him there? Maybe Lauren was protecting Shawn from becoming too attached to him. Whatever her reasoning, he still missed them.

Sleep didn't come easily. All he could think about

was seeing Lauren the next day. How would she react? Would there be that uncomfortable moment when neither of them knew what to say? She was the one person he had found he had no trouble discussing things with, including his fiasco with Gabriella. He still couldn't believe he told her that entire sordid story.

Monday morning when she arrived at the clinic he was busy in his office. With great effort he waited until she'd hung up her coat and come in search of him. That was one of the favorite parts of his day. Lauren seemed eager to see him, whereas Gabriella had always impatiently expected him to wait on her or be on her schedule. He'd always been an afterthought to her. Lauren made him a priority. She believed in him and therefore he believed in himself. Making him feel as if her day hadn't started until she saw him.

She hesitated in the doorway, as she always did. Paxton glanced up then back at the laptop. Confident she couldn't resist knowing what was on the screen, he waited until she circled the desk before closing the top and standing. His arm slipped around her waist, pulling her tightly to him. "I thought you'd never get here." He kissed her thoroughly. As he did, he turned her, lifted her and seated her on the desk.

She broke their kiss with a laugh.

He didn't have to worry about that uncomfortable moment any longer. Looking down at her, he asked with all the innocence he could muster, "Something wrong?"

"I was just thinking I used to play under this desk when I was a kid."

He wiggled his eyebrows up and down like a movie villain. "Now you're getting to play on it."

She giggled, placed a hand at the nape of his neck and brought his mouth back to hers. His fingers slipped under her shirt and sweater to find her warm skin. Lauren cooed her pleasure. This was a great way to start the morning.

The ring of the bell on the door jarred them apart. They both snickered into each other's necks.

"You almost got caught," he whispered in her ear as if she had been the only one to blame.

Lauren gave him a swat on the shoulder.

With a quick kiss, he helped her off the desk.

"I'll be right there," she called, straightening her clothes.

Giving her a direct look, he mouthed, "I'll be out when I can."

Lauren glanced at his crotch and grinned. She said too sweetly, like a nurse in a bad sitcom, "Yes, Doctor."

Paxton watched the sway of her hips as she left the office. That didn't help ease his pain. In Boston, he would never have dared, much less thought about sneaking a kiss from his lover at work. A Samuels didn't act that way. It was fun being naughty.

As their patient closed the door on her way out, Lauren turned to Paxton. "We're lucky Mrs. Betts's hearing has gone because she used to be the worst gossip in town."

He chuckled and pulled her in for a hug. "Would it be so bad to have people talking about us?" Paxton couldn't believe he'd just asked that. After living with concern over what people thought all his life, now he didn't care. It was a freeing idea.

Lauren gave him a long look. "It wouldn't be the first time." She shrugged. "And it would be true."

Paxton gave her a kiss. "It would be." So why had he been so uptight about the gossip in Boston when his wedding had come crashing down? He hadn't done anything wrong. Except to ask the wrong woman to marry him. He owed nobody an explanation of who he saw and what he did. His feelings for Lauren he didn't mind anyone knowing. In fact, he wanted to announce it to everyone he was going to see today. He wouldn't do that because he wasn't staying in Last Stop. She shouldn't have to answer a bunch of questions about their relationship.

The rest of the day moved along as usual, except he smiled more than normal. Lauren left at closing time, saying bye with a quick kiss. It was quiet afterward, too much so. He missed her already. What was he going to do when he returned to Boston? Could he ask her to leave everything she knew and come to Boston? That would be flipping her world and Shawn's on their sides.

Still, it would tear his heart out when he had to leave them behind. For now he had at least two more weeks before he was to leave and until then he was going to enjoy himself, and Lauren, to the fullest. The future he would worry about later.

Lauren hadn't suggested they have dinner together but neither had he. Pulling a casserole out of his freezer, he headed for her house. He walked so that his car parked outside wouldn't create any gossip. Old ideas died hard.

When he knocked he didn't have to wait long before Lauren opened the door with a smile. "What took you so long?"

He grinned. "You were expecting me?"

"Oh, about thirty minutes ago."

"Well, Miss Smarty Pants, watch out. I might surprise you and take my frozen meal elsewhere."

"Please don't do that. I was looking forward to seeing what you showed up with tonight," she pleaded playfully.

"Well, since you insist, sure! I'll have dinner with you." He stepped inside and headed down the hallway toward the kitchen.

She laughed, closed the door and followed. "Surely there's an end to these."

"I think this is the last of them." Paxton placed the casserole on the stove.

"You may have to start cooking."

He kissed her. "I was hoping maybe you would take pity on me and cook."

She pushed him away. "You only want me for my cooking skills."

Paxton grabbed her bottom with one hand and kissed her again. "Among other things."

Shawn sat in the middle of the floor, playing with a pot and wooden spoon. Paxton swung him up into his arms. The boy giggled. Something about being with the two of them seemed right. He belonged here.

"Would you mind watching Shawn while dinner warms so I can get a couple of things done?"

"I can do that." Only a few days ago Paxton would

have hesitated at first. What type of spell had Lauren cast over him? This was the closest to feeling like a member of a family he'd ever experienced.

After dinner Paxton washed up while Lauren bathed Shawn. Paxton wasn't particularly confident in his ability to do dishes—he had a dishwasher and someone come over to clean his place every week—but he vowed to give it a try. Lauren had enough to do.

With them cleared to the best of his ability, he now stood in the doorway of Shawn's room, watching Lauren read "A Visit from St. Nicholas" to the sleepy boy. As he did, a peace he'd never known before settled over him. This was a precious moment and he was a part of it.

"'And to all a good night.'" Lauren closed the book, kissed her sleeping son and came to join him.

Hugging her close, he kissed her on top of the head. "Nice kid."

"Yeah, he is."

They stood there for a while then Lauren headed out of the room and Paxton left the door open a crack. Could he be a father? Did he want to be? Just days ago he would have said no but after meeting Lauren...

She started toward the kitchen. "There's not much entertainment I can offer you. TV, a movie, cards or puzzle."

Paxton had other ideas about how to spend their evening, but he enjoyed her company in and out of bed and he wanted Lauren to know that. "How about a puzzle?" He couldn't remember the last time he had put one together.

As she entered the kitchen she said, "Wow, you cleaned up."

Paxton puffed out his chest as if he'd won a sporting event. "I did. I'm not sure how good a job I did but I tried."

Wearing a small smile, Lauren narrowed her eyes. "First time?"

"Uh…" He winced. "Yeah."

She strolled to him, kissing him on the cheek. "It's perfect."

Her kiss and approval was the best reward his efforts had ever earned.

"The puzzles are in a cabinet over here." She moved across the room and opened a door, revealing three shelves packed with boxes.

"Wow."

Lauren shrugged. "The nights get long here in the winter. So, what'll you have? Hundred, five hundred or a thousand pieces?"

"How about we start with a hundred? I'm not sure I've done a puzzle since I was in grade school."

Lauren looked at him. "Really? How sad."

He couldn't disagree with her.

"So why did you say you wanted to do one?"

"Sounded fun. I'm learning to have fun." She might not know it, but she was teaching him.

"I like fun." She pulled a box out. "This is one of my favorites."

He recognized the picture of the Grand Canal in Venice. "Why's this your favorite?"

"I've just always thought I'd like to go there someday." She put the puzzle box on the table and opened it.

"I've been. It's beautiful. As pretty as this picture." His parents had given him a chance to see the world.

They had traveled as a family when his father had gone to medical conferences. Maybe his parents had been better than he had given them credit for. They *had* offered him some amazing opportunities.

"I'd love to visit someday." She dumped the pieces on the table. "I've had this puzzle since I was a child."

So she'd been dreaming of going for a long time. He'd love to show her the city. But that wouldn't be. What they had was now and a few more days.

Lauren couldn't believe that Paxton was actually into completing the puzzle. They worked together, laughing when one tried to get a piece in where the other wanted to place theirs. They stopped long enough to have a hot drink.

"I hope I'm not making a mistake in asking, but I accidentally overheard part of your conversation with your mom the other day. What is going on?"

A dark shadow filled Paxton's eyes. He took a sip of his drink and put the mug on the table before he answered. "They want me to come home right now. Dad's ill and has gotten worse, Mother is worried. They are pushing me to return to Boston."

She took his hand and laced her fingers in his. "If you need to go, go. We will make do until we find another doctor."

Paxton shook his head. "I meet my obligations. I promised to be here until the end of the month and that's what I plan to do."

Unwilling to start an argument with him, Lauren let the subject drop. They returned to the puzzle. Down to the last piece, they discovered that it was missing. She panicked. Where could it be? She was always so careful not to lose any.

"Let's look around," Paxton said in a calm, clear voice. "It has to be here somewhere."

She went down on her hands and knees under the table to search the floor.

"Hey, I found it," Paxton called.

She stood in time to see him lock the last piece in place. "Where did you find it?"

"In my pocket." He gave her an innocent, mischievous look.

"Oh, you." She went after him with a smile on her face. "You did that on purpose."

He grabbed her flailing arms and pulled her to him. "How else was I going to get to enjoy you wiggling your cute butt when you climbed under the table?"

She glared at him. He looked so adorable and relaxed. "You know I'll have to get even, don't you?"

Paxton stood, letting her slide over the hard length of him. "Honey, I was counting on that." His mouth found hers for a deep, hot kiss.

Just before daylight he slipped out of her bed to go home. Lauren hated losing his warmth.

On Wednesday when it was time to close for the day, she was looking forward to spending time with Shawn. As happy as she was with Paxton, she would not neglect her son. Paxton had yet to say anything about them spending the afternoon together. Before she left, she went in search of him, finding him in his lab.

"Hey, I'm leaving," she announced as she entered the tiny lab. "Mom's expecting me to get Shawn." She put her arm across Paxton's shoulders and kissed him. Things were so easy between them.

"You're leaving?" He seemed surprised she was there.

"You know, if I had less self-esteem I might be jealous of this lab where you're always examining something."

Wrapping an arm about her waist, he pulled her into his lap and gave her a deep sizzling kiss. As he nuzzled her neck he said, "I wouldn't mind examining you."

"As nice as that sounds, I have to pick up Shawn." Could life get any better than being held by Paxton?

"What do you have planned for this afternoon?"

"I've got to run to Lippscomb. Get a couple of Christmas gifts I couldn't find online."

He made a negative sound. "More shopping." He sighed, only to brighten a moment later. "Lauren, I know you like to spend time with Shawn on Wednesdays, but why don't you let me go pick him up and have him at your place when you get back? That way he can have a nap and I'll even plan supper tonight."

Lauren leaned back and looked at him. "Are you sure? He can be a handful."

"I'm sure. You'll get your shopping done faster and I'll get more time with you."

She hesitated for a second. *Was this a good idea?* Could this be the same guy who had hesitated to hold Shawn not long ago? But he was right, she could finish her shopping a lot faster without a two-year-old along. Her mother already helped her out enough so Lauren didn't want to ask her to do more. Finally she said, "Okay, I guess. I'll call Mom and let her know you're coming."

Fifteen minutes later she was on her way to Lippscomb, unsure if she'd made the correct decision. She hoped Paxton hadn't bitten off more than he could chew by volunteering to watch Shawn. Deepening her uncertainty was the uncomfortable conviction she'd already become far too attached to Paxton. She didn't want Shawn troubled when Paxton left. It filled her heart with joy that Paxton had offered to babysit. He knew the way to a mother's heart.

Still, the fear that he might not stay niggled at her. She'd been hurt before. Last Stop was her home, her safe place. She wanted Shawn to have the feeling of security that growing up in a small town would give him. When she'd married Mark, it had been exciting to leave this tiny burg behind, but she had no interest in repeating that mistake. It hadn't taken her long to learn that Last Stop hadn't been as bad as she'd thought it was.

She and Paxton lived in two different worlds. She'd experienced some of his world and it hadn't been for her after all. Even so, she couldn't ignore the obvious. Paxton wasn't Mark. Their relationship was completely different from the one she'd had with her husband. Paxton seemed at home in Last Stop. Mark had been an outsider and that had never changed.

CHAPTER NINE

A FEW HOURS later Lauren pulled into her drive, wondering what to expect. At least the house was still standing. What would the inside look like? She entered through the back door. All was quiet. To her amazement there was a wonderful smell coming from the oven. Another casserole, she was sure. She continued down the hallway. Nothing. Shawn and Paxton were here somewhere because his car was outside.

When she came to her bedroom she glanced in. Paxton lay on the bed with Shawn curled up next to him, and both were sound asleep. Transfixed by the endearing sight, her heart swelled. Heaven help her, she was in love. With vision blurred by tears, she quietly returned to the kitchen.

The creak of the floor warned her someone was there a second before strong arms circled her waist and pulled her back against an unyielding chest.

Paxton kissed her neck. "Hey, get everything done?"

Covertly wiping the wetness from her eyes by rubbing them with thumb and forefinger, she turned without breaking his embrace and smiled. "I sure did. How'd it go here?"

"Good. Shawn and I did just fine."

"Really?"

"It might have been rocky there for a few minutes but we men came to an understanding." Paxton acted as if he'd achieved an award. "Dinner will be ready when Shawn wakes up."

"Sounds good."

"Any ideas what we can do while we wait?" Paxton's hands caressed her back.

"We could watch TV." Lauren didn't look him in the eyes in an effort to cover the emotion still filling her chest. He'd be gone soon and her heart would go with him.

"I tell you what, you watch while I nibble on you." Paxton gave her a hungry kiss that she eagerly returned.

Half an hour later Shawn was up. He was happy to see her but he gravitated back toward Paxton the moment he was done hugging her. Paxton and Shawn had become buddies. That wasn't good. Now there would be two hurting when the time came. Yet she couldn't push Paxton away.

Paxton had her sit while he served dinner. With great fanfare, he removed a large pan from the oven containing roasted beef, potatoes and vegetables. He set a plate of rolls on the table.

She grinned. "How did you know I love the café's roast beef and potatoes?"

Paxton lifted a shoulder. "What can I say, it pays to know the cook."

When he settled into the chair beside her she leaned over and kissed him. "Thank you for this. It's nice."

"You're welcome." He was a man very satisfied with himself.

They were almost through with their meal when Paxton said, "Your mother invited me to lunch Saturday."

Lauren's heart caught. She had been tempted to ask him herself but had refrained from doing so out of fear he wouldn't feel comfortable. She feared that it might be too much too soon. After hearing his stark description of his family's Christmas celebrations, she wasn't at all sure he would appreciate the simplicity of hers. "Are you coming?"

"Sure. What I wondered was why you hadn't invited me?"

She placed her hand over his. "I just wasn't sure you would want to. My family get-togethers can be loud, and that's putting it mildly. It's not something you are used to."

"Don't worry, I can handle it." He raised his head with complete confidence.

On Saturday afternoon, as they approached Lauren's parents' home, Paxton asked, "So who will be here today?"

"My brothers, their wives and children, my grandparents, a few cousins and some neighbors. The usual."

"All at your parents' house?"

"Sure. It's our family home. My grandparents used to live there but now live in a retirement community in Lippscomb. Before them were my great-grandparents. Before them great-great-grandparents who homesteaded it."

"Homesteaded? Like the Oklahoma land rush?" And his family acted as if they had cornered history.

"Something like that. A couple of my male ancestors rode out here from the east. They wrote home to say the grass was as high as a horse's belly, to come on out, that there was land to be had. They did."

"The law was that you had to sleep on your land for a certain amount of time, so they built a simple sod house. One built out of large squares of dirt. As I'm sure you have noticed, we don't have many trees. Anyway, they built at the corner of four sections."

"Sections?" Paxton was fascinated.

Lauren's pride in her heritage clearly came through in her every word. "One mile by one mile square, or six hundred and forty acres."

"I vaguely remember studying that in school." The moment in history had been a paragraph in a textbook.

"Out here we live by it. Have you paid any attention to how the roads run?"

He had, but had never thought to ask why. In Boston, there was no rhyme or reason to the streets and alleys. Here they had been mapped out.

"Anyway, a different member of the family slept in a different room in each corner of the house so that they could file for all four of the sections."

"That's a lot of land. Two thousand, five hundred and sixty acres!"

"Yeah, but to put it into perspective, in your part of the country you can feed fifty cows on an acre while here we feed one cow on fifty acres."

"That's a big difference." There were many of those between them. But that was what he liked most about her. She wasn't a carbon copy of the next woman.

"It takes more land out here, but I love these wide open spaces." She turned into her parents' drive.

When they entered the house, her mother promptly emerged from the kitchen, wiping her hands on her apron, and welcomed them.

"Thanks for having me," Paxton said in greeting.

Mrs. Tucker hugged him. "We're glad you could come. Lauren, be sure to introduce Paxton to everyone."

His own mother had never shown that much emotion when he'd entered a room.

Lauren made sure he met her brothers and their families. Both lived in surrounding counties and were farmers as well. Despite them giving him a narrow-eyed look, implying they were watching him closely, Paxton like them instantly. They had strong handshakes and were men who obviously loved and cherished their families.

The kitchen counters were loaded with food. A long wide table was set with what must have been Mrs. Tucker's best china and glassware. Nearby a smaller table sat that looked like a miniature of the larger one. He guessed it was for the children.

Lauren's father called the group to order around the enormous table. Paxton stood behind Lauren, who held Shawn. As her father continued to speak Shawn began to squirm. Paxton reached around her, taking the boy. He quieted. Looking up, he saw there was more than one set of eyes watching him. Their expressions ran the gambit between surprised to soft approving smiles on the women's faces. He had stepped through another door that was going to make his leaving even more difficult.

Mr. Tucker said the blessing. Everyone filed by the food, filling their plates. Lauren served his plate while he held Shawn. She led them to a spot at the table with a highchair. Paxton slipped Shawn into place.

"You're pretty good at that," one of her brothers stated in a flat tone.

"I've had some practice now. You should have seen me with the stroller for the first time."

Her other brother piped up, "You wait until you dress a kid for the first time. Emily had her dress on backward when I got through." They all laughed.

"So Paxton, do you follow football?" Mr. Tucker asked.

"I do. Boston College and the New England Patriots."

From there the conversation turned to sports and became loud and animated.

With dinner finished, the family gathered around the Christmas tree. Paxton whispered to Lauren, "I didn't bring something for everyone."

"Don't worry. We all draw names for one person and bring presents only for the children. I've taken care of it."

He was sure she had. Lauren had a way of doing that. His family's Christmases were sedate and proper, while Lauren's was filled with shouts and affectionate hugs. He was fascinated, enthralled and included. He hadn't expected to receive a present, but there was one for him under the tree. It was from Lauren's parents. It was a knit blanket decorated with different places of importance in Last Stop like the oil refinery, Main Street, the church and others. He looked at Lauren's mother, almost too moved to respond, but at the last moment managed to say gratefully, "Thank you."

"I thought you could use something to remember us by," she said.

Paxton looked at Lauren. Forgetting them wouldn't be possible. It had been the best family Christmas celebration he'd ever been involved in.

Lauren slipped out of the comfortable bed, leaving the heat of Paxton to see that Christmas was all in place for Shawn. Even though he was young she wanted him to experience it all. She was just pulling the presents out of the closet when she felt Paxton's arms around her. She would have known it was him even with her eyes closed. His touch had been ingrained in her by now. She would miss it terribly when he was gone but that she would think about later. Today would be a happy one.

"Hey, I missed you." His drowsy voice was rough and sensual.

She turned in his arms. Clad only in jeans, his naked torso warmed her. "Merry Christmas."

"Best one I've ever had. I like finding such a sexy elf slipping around the room." He kissed her.

Lauren giggled. "Since you're up you can help me." She handed him the bag. "Shawn will be awake in a few minutes."

Together they arranged the presents under the tree. They had just finished when her son's sleepy call rang out. With a quick glance at the tree, Lauren hurried to get him. She soon returned with a huge smile on her face. Shawn looked at the lit tree surrounded by gifts and toys in wonderment.

"Look, baby, Santa came to see us," she cooed as her toddler rubbed sleep from his eyes.

Paxton stood to the side, as if he didn't want to interrupt the moment and was feeling out of place.

Lauren glanced at him with glistening eyes and a beaming smile. She waved him to her. His smile covered his face as he slid an arm around her waist. Moments later Shawn was on the floor, with Lauren and Paxton crouched beside him as he tried to tear open a present. He was more interested in the paper than the gift.

She picked up a package out from under the tree and offered it to Paxton. "This is for you."

Paxton looked both shocked and pleased. He opened it. Inside was a book about the history of the area.

She stood and came close. "I thought you might like it." There was a hint of hesitation in her words.

He hugged her. "I can hardly wait to read it. After being here, I'll know the places I'm reading about. I have something for you." Paxton tucked the book under his arm, went to the tree and picked up a large beribboned box.

Lauren felt more than she could put words to as she accepted the gift. Paxton had thought to get her something. When and how had he gotten it into her home and under her tree without her noticing? Sitting on the couch, she placed the present in her lap. Savoring the anticipation, she pulled the ribbon off.

"Do you always open a gift so slowly?" Exasperation was clear in Paxton's voice.

She looked at him. "I do that when it's something special." Lauren lifted the top off to find a bright orange teapot and matching cups and saucers nestled in yellow tissue paper. She lifted the pot out. Moving it one direction then the other, she examined it at eye level. It was wonderful. Paxton knew enough about her to know that it would be perfect in her kitchen. Meeting Paxton's questioning gaze, she declared, "I love them."

He grinned, looking boyishly proud of himself.

Setting the pot back in the box, Lauren patted the seat next to her. He moved to sit beside her. She gave him a kiss, hoping to convey all the love she felt.

A few hours later they were preparing to leave the house when Paxton's phone rang. He looked more resigned than pleased when he checked to see who was calling.

"It's my mom. I need to get this."

"Of course you do. I'll take Shawn to the kitchen."

"No. Stay right here."

It was as if he needed a lifeline and she was it. He sat on the bed and had her sit close as Shawn played at their feet.

Paxton answered. "Merry Christmas, Mom, Dad."

"Hi, son." A deep male voice traveled through the phone, surprisingly loud.

"Hello, Paxton," came a cool female one.

"How are you spending the day today?" his father asked.

"I'm with Lauren and her son Shawn," Paxton answered.

His mother's voice came across the line. "You haven't become involved with some woman out there, have you?"

Lauren couldn't help but tense.

"Lauren and I are friends. She's my nurse and has been kind enough to share her Christmas with me." Paxton's hand squeezed hers.

His friend.

That's right. That's all they were and would really ever be.

"When do you plan to be home?" his father asked.

"In a week."

"Can't you be here sooner than that? After all, we have the big New Year event at the club," his mother stated.

"Paxton," his father said. "I really need you here. You shouldn't have left anyway."

Lauren watched Paxton closely. How would she feel if her father was sick and she was so far away?

"I'll be home as soon as I can. Thanks for calling. Merry Christmas." Paxton hung up.

Lauren glanced at him. A dark expression covered his face. She watched him but said nothing.

"They just wanted to wish me a Merry Christmas." Paxton's nonchalance implied it was no big deal but Lauren suspected that wasn't the case. And they had not once wished him a Merry Christmas or told him that they missed him.

"If you need to go home, people will understand. I would. It sounds like your parents need you."

"Let's not talk about it today." Paxton's tone indicated that was final.

They quietly finished dressing. By the time he was loading Shawn into her car Paxton's good nature had returned. The rest of the day was spent going to church, visiting her parents and a few friends. It ended with Shawn sleeping soundly and Lauren and Paxton huddled on the sofa in the dark, looking at the Christmas-tree lights.

Lauren couldn't remember a more wonderful Christmas. Filled with family, laughter and Paxton.

CHAPTER TEN

BEFORE SUNRISE THE next morning Lauren woke to Paxton's hand brushing her mid-section. Sweet tingles ran over her and heat filled her center. His slightest touch made her feel alive. He dropped kisses along her jaw then found her mouth before he rose over her. She was waiting to welcome him.

Later Lauren watched him dress. If only she could have this every day. Her heart jolted. What was she doing? Repeating history. And not happy history. The kind that left her with a broken heart. Another handsome, intelligent man had come to town and whisked her off her feet. Heartache and devastation would be left in his wake.

Lauren climbed out of bed. She should be clothed to have this conversation with Paxton. Pulling on her robe as if arming herself, she brought the collar up around her face.

She'd allowed Paxton to become a personal part of her life. To go to her parents' house on a holiday like they were a couple and, worse, let her precious son get to know him. Moisture filled her eyes. Her heart hurt. She knew what she had to do. But could she? She wanted to eke out every single second she could have with him but this had to stop before it went any further. Heaven help her, it was already out of hand. It couldn't continue. More kisses, more touches, more of Paxton would only make it harder.

Paxton didn't look at her as he spoke. "I have to leave right after New Year's, so why don't we celebrate on Friday?"

He'd asked so nonchalantly. Didn't he know he was slowly killing her? She took so long to answer that Paxton glanced at her. "I don't think so. My brother has been begging me to bring Shawn for a visit for a few days. I thought this week would be a good time to go since you're here to cover the clinic and it's really slow between the holidays."

Paxton faced her and glared in disbelief, his shirt half-buttoned.

She loved his chest. *Focus.* The only way to survive this was to concentrate.

"You do know I'm leaving on Saturday? I have to be at work at the clinic in Boston on January the second. I'd hoped we'd spend as much of the next few days together as possible."

"To what end?"

He looked as if she had struck him. "I'm not sure how to respond to that."

"Look, things happened fast between us. We knew it wasn't going to last. Last Stop is my home. Boston is yours. We both understood that, going in. It has been wonderful. I'll always remember you. You are an amazing man." She sounded far cooler than she felt. It was becoming hard to breathe.

"Well, you seem to have given this a lot of thought.

I'm glad I could be of service this morning before you dropped the bomb on me."

Now they were both going down an ugly road. Lauren swallowed. "I'm sorry you feel that way. This morning was beautiful. I'll treasure each moment we spent together." *And relive them in my dreams, cry over them into my pillow.*

Paxton raised a pleading hand. "Lauren, can't we…?"

She shook her head. "It won't make it any better. You have obligations in Boston. Your father needs you. You're the kind of guy who doesn't let people down."

"I don't want this to end. Couldn't you come to Boston sometimes? Maybe I could get out here. Or we could meet halfway."

Lauren pursed her lips and shook her head. "I couldn't do that to Shawn. He deserves better than a mother who dumps him on his grandparents for a weekend of sex."

Paxton made a face and swung his head. "Come on, Lauren, you know it's more than that."

"How would I know that? You've never said anything about wanting more." A stricken look came over his face. He ran his hand over his hair, messing it more. At another time, during another discussion she would have reached over and moved a lock off his forehead. "I just think it's time to end this fling. I thought it would be easier on us both to say goodbye now and not have to see each other every day."

His face paled. "Are you running away, Lauren?"

This time it was her turn to feel as if she'd been hit. She *was* running, but it was the only way she knew to keep from crumbling at his feet and begging him not to go—ever. "I'm not doing anything you haven't done."

He winced. The pain in his face had her wanting to reach out to him, but she held herself in check. Had she gone too far?

"You're right, I did run. But you did the same thing. You wanted to get out of Last Stop, and you took off running the first chance you got, with the first guy that could get you out of town. What's more, at the first sign of trouble you came running back."

She leaned toward him, her face screwed up. "I had Shawn to think about."

"An excuse. You are a smart, creative and resourceful woman. You could live anywhere. But you hide out here because it's easy, safe. You have no room to criticize me."

Anger welled in her. How dared he analyze her life when he couldn't handle his own? "And your problem is you have let your obligation to your father and family control your life. I understand you love your parents. I do too. But you are a great doctor, capable of providing excellent care anywhere, be that in Boston or somewhere else in the world. I think you deserve to be happy where you work. I'm going to take a wild guess here and say that isn't in Boston. The question is, do you know what you want? *Really* want? I don't think you'll ever be happy until you figure that out."

Paxton couldn't believe what he was hearing. Was that really his problem? How Lauren saw him? As being unable to stand up for himself, know what he wanted? Maybe he didn't know. Was that why he couldn't be completely happy in his work in Boston?

The need to take the offensive filled him. "Loyalty is important to me. I was raised to believe that came before everything." Even what he wanted. "Apparently you don't have any trouble analyzing my issues but you can't seem to see your own. What I do know is that there's a great big world out there and you're hiding in Last Stop because you're afraid of getting hurt again. You need to decide whether or not you're here because it's where you want to be or whether it's because you're too scared to try and make it without the security of what you've known all your life."

Lauren threw back her shoulders and in a snide, haughty tone said, "Well, it seems that we both have our issues. Since you're leaving in four days to deal with yours—" she waved a hand between them "—I think my plan to go to my brother's is a good one. Bye, Paxton. Have a good life. It's been nice knowing you."

Lauren stalked out of the room and turned toward the kitchen, leaving him with the sick feeling that his chance at lifelong happiness had gone with her.

A few days later Paxton drove out of Last Stop with a heavy heart. He hadn't seen Lauren since their fight. He'd been miserable but hadn't known how he could change things. He was who he was and she was who she was. Still, the feeling that he was leaving behind something central to his living and breathing dogged him. Sadly, he was confident he knew what it was. What he didn't know was what to do about it.

In Last Stop, Paxton had discovered he could describe his life as fun. *Fun*. He'd never thought about it before but now that he'd had a taste of it, he wanted it to continue. All the time. From an accident, an awkward stay in a hotel, the massive amounts of food he'd been given, his secret with Mr. Gerhart, finding out he was jealous of a two-year-old, a Christmas parade, a kiss under the mistletoe, all the dinners with Lauren and Shawn, and most of all nights with Lauren had all come together to make his life enjoyable. For the first time he'd known genuine happiness.

Christmas with Lauren in Last Stop had been more fulfilling and memorable than he'd imagined any holiday could be. Outside of his parents' call, which had put a momentary dampener on the day, it had been perfect. Now he was leaving all that behind.

Instead of sharing New Year's Eve with Lauren in his arms, Paxton had heard the fireworks from inside his little lab. He'd felt no joy. If he'd believed his life had been depressing after the fiasco with Gabriella, it didn't compare to how he felt now.

On the straight highway out of town, with dark clouds gathering in the west that could only mean more snow, he pressed the gas pedal to the floor, making the sports car fly along the road. All he wanted to do was drive so fast he could forget how much his heart was breaking.

He arrived in Boston exhausted, but with a decision made. He'd rolled over, mulled, examined and contemplated everything Lauren had said as he'd traveled. As much as he hated to admit it, she was right. He was holding on to something he didn't want and for all the wrong reasons.

She had said that he didn't know what he really wanted. Now he did. He had to make his parents understand that the path they had planned for him wasn't his destiny. His father had good medical care, extended family around him and Paxton being there wasn't going to make his disease go away. The Samuels Clinic wasn't where he needed to be. He was required elsewhere.

He'd felt more love and had had more devotion and support than he'd ever had before from Lauren. He wanted that for the rest of his life. Life might have forced him into changes but he was going to embrace them and find that happiness again that he'd known so briefly. His first order of business was to close up his life in Boston.

Returning to work at the clinic that had his family name across the entrance the next morning, Paxton drafted a resignation letter. With that complete, he wrote a letter that would go out to all his patients, explaining he would no longer be practicing in Boston.

The next item on his list was to speak to his parents. Knowing they could be found at the club that night and that they would insist he come there to talk, he dressed in a suit, which reminded him of the first night he'd made love to Lauren. Would she listen to him when he returned to Last Stop?

Paxton entered the club with his head held high. He wasn't the person who should be ashamed. He located his parents in the dining room. His father stood as Paxton approached and shook his hand. He did look more fragile but Paxton couldn't let his father's health control his own happiness. He kissed his mother's offered cheek.

"I didn't expect to see you this evening. I'm glad you are back," his mother said as he took a seat beside her. "We have to start planning the fundraiser soon if we're going to get everything done."

"I'm going to have nothing to do with that. I'm only back in town long enough to pack up."

"What?" His father's voice carried a note of concern.

"I resigned today. I'm leaving Boston." Paxton couldn't believe how good it felt to say it.

"You can't do that," his mother said in a high voice. "Your place is here. Your father needs you."

"It's already done. I'll be leaving in under two weeks." Paxton didn't waver despite the look of distress on his mother's face.

"Why are you doing this to us?" His mother pulled the cloth napkins between her hands.

"I'm not doing anything to you, Mother. I'm finding the right place for me. Where I want to be." He hoped to set up his practice in Last Stop. If not there, then somewhere that he could be his own man. Whatever happened between him and Lauren, it was time he went out on his own.

"I've never understood you, son," his mother whined.

"I know, Mom. I wish you did. I've discovered what'll make me happy. I'm going after it."

"What is that?" His father sounded genuinely interested in his answer for the first time in years.

"I want a small practice where I know everyone by their first names. Where I can watch the children grow up. Where I'm part of the community for who I am and not because of my name. I want to feel needed."

His father nodded then asked, "You can't find that

here? The position on the board will give you power to do things you can't do now."

Paxton looked around the room. "No, I can't. I'm sorry I can't be here for you, Dad. I love you but I can't take your place and I don't want to. Retire. Enjoy your life."

His mother broke in. "We've always loved and supported you. How can you do this to us? If you and Gabriella could work things out—"

"That isn't going to happen. As for support, you have only done that if it's what you wanted me to do. It's time I do what makes me happy and not try to fit the mold you've created for me."

"Where'll you go?" his father asked.

"Back to Last Stop if I can. Somewhere like it, if not there."

"You would leave everything you have here to live in a nowhere place like that?" His mother sounded appalled at the idea.

"Yes, I would." Paxton stood. "Well, I'll be going. I have a lot to organize. I'll come by the house to say goodbye before I leave."

Paxton left with a weight he'd had no idea he'd been carrying lifted from his shoulders.

Lauren was aware she was making herself sick but had no idea how to do anything different. She was heartsick and the only remedy for that she knew of was time. Each day was about going through the motions. The only area she wasn't failing in was taking care of Shawn.

The days she was at her brother's had been bitter-sweet. It was nice to visit with her family but all she had wanted to do was run back to Paxton. The day he'd left she'd stayed in her room and cried. Her brother and sister-in-law had seen to Shawn and let her alone. She missed him with an ache that throbbed continuously. It was only because of Shawn she believed she might survive.

She and Paxton had said some hateful things to each other. Some she believed Paxton had needed to hear. But he'd done the same to her. At the time she hadn't thought they were true, but now she was questioning that. Was she hiding out in Last Stop or was it really where she wanted to be?

For years she'd dreamed of leaving. When she'd gotten the chance and found the outside world wasn't all that grand she had run home. But that didn't make her and Paxton's situation the same. Or did it? Was she letting her past dictate her future, too?

Paxton had been gone two days when Lauren drove out to her parents' house.

Her mother took one look at her, took Shawn and put him down to play, then gave Lauren a tight hug. "Have a seat. I'll fix us something hot to drink then you can tell me all about it."

Her mother always knew when Lauren needed to talk. Even when she'd told her parents she was marrying Mark and leaving with him they had been supportive. Maybe not happy but supportive. She knew her parents were there for her, which was something Paxton had never felt from his. That was sad and wrong.

A few minutes later her mother put a mug in front of Lauren and then took a seat with her own in her hand.

"Mom, do you thinking I'm hiding out in Last

Stop? That I'm too scared to do something else? That I ran back here?"

Her mother gave her a thoughtful look. "Some."

Lauren was shocked at her answer. She really hadn't expected her mother to agree with Paxton.

Her mother continued, "I knew most of your life you wanted to get out of Last Stop. It was all you talked about. I wasn't surprised that you took the first chance you had. Your father and I weren't enamored with Mark but you seemed to love him and we could accept that. It made sense that you came home because of Shawn. You needed the help. But you never spoke of leaving again. As eager as you were to leave the first time, it seemed odd you never talked of going elsewhere, not even moving to Lippscomb. I have to admit I'm glad to have you and Shawn close so I never asked what happened."

So her mother had noticed.

"As time went by I saw you isolate yourself more. It became Shawn and you. You didn't go on dates. I know you were asked." She grinned. "After all, this is a small town. I have to say I was starting to think you'd never take a chance again. Then Paxton came to town."

"You know?"

"Honey, if it hadn't been written on your face every time you looked at him then I would have heard. You love him, don't you?"

"Yes."

"Then what's wrong? Go after him. It doesn't matter where you live as long as you're together. Step out and see the world again. This time I'd bet true love is waiting for you."

"What if he doesn't want me? I said some awful things to him."

Her mother cocked her head to one side. "What if he does and you don't tell him?"

"I can't just pick up and go to Boston." Lauren looked down at Shawn.

"Why not?"

"There's Shawn, the clinic…" Lauren's heart was beating faster at the possibility.

"Your dad and I will keep Shawn. People have managed around here before without the clinic being open," her mother said.

What if Paxton refused to talk to her? What if she didn't fit in in Boston? Could she do this? What would happen if she didn't? Her heart would never survive. That answered all her questions.

Lauren hugged her mother. "I have an airline ticket to buy."

Paxton was finishing up on the last of the boxes holding his belongings when the doorbell of his apartment rang. He made a small sound of disgust, fearing it was his mother. She'd called almost daily, asking him to reconsider leaving. Her interest unnerved him. He'd not had her razor-edged focus to this degree since he was a child. Was she now making a house call?

Dressed in a button-down shirt and jeans, which he'd taken to wearing more often than not, he went to the door. He opened it with negative words on his lips that he quickly swallowed. His heart did a tap dance in his chest.

Lauren stood there. A more beautiful sight he'd never seen. Her eyes were wide with uncertainty.

Her gorgeous hair down around her shoulders. She watched him a moment as if judging her reception.

"Hi, Paxton."

Her soft Western drawl was music to his ears. She'd said the words as if she came to his door regularly.

For a moment he stood speechless with disbelief. Was she really there? He'd dreamed of her nightly. She was like water to his thirsty soul. He managed to sputter, "I wasn't expecting *you*."

"I was afraid if I called you might not see me. I want to apologize."

Paxton suddenly registered they were standing in his doorway. He reached out a hand to touch her but stopped himself. If he did he would have her in his arms whether she liked it or not. "Come in."

She did and he closed the door behind them with a shaking hand. He hadn't been this nervous since he'd seen his first patient by himself. This was his chance to get what he dreamed of in life. He couldn't mess it up. Wouldn't.

"You're moving?" Lauren looked around the room.

"I am." The question of where hung in the air. For him that depended on her.

She turned to face him. "Look, Paxton, I'm sorry for all those horrible things I said to you. You were right, I had no right to talk about your choices in life when I had my own problems. You're a grown man who can handle his relationships without my help."

But he hadn't been able to until now. She'd shown him that. "You came all this way to tell me that?"

"I did. And to get out of Last Stop for a little while. I needed to see if I could do it. Even for a few days."

"And how has that gone for you?" They stood so

close yet he hadn't touched her. His hands shook at the thought. Fear held him immobile. He watched her.

"Better than I thought. I've been thinking lately I need to get out more. Move away from Last Stop. There are other places that might work better for Shawn and me."

Paxton wanted her in Last Stop but if she wanted to leave he'd ask if he could follow. "Like?"

She gave her signature shrug. "I was thinking Boston."

That was all he needed to hear. Paxton grinned and stepped into her personal space. He wasn't surprised when Lauren didn't move. He looked into her eyes. All deep, warm and welcoming. "Why's that?"

She softly said, "Because this is where *you* are."

"And that matters to you?" Paxton's hands held her elbows. He didn't miss the shiver that ran through her.

"Yes. Very much."

"Why?" He needed to hear her say the words. With his history he had to know she truly cared.

Her hands came to his chest. "Because I love you. I want to be with you. Here or anywhere else you go."

Paxton swooped her into his arms and kissed her deeply, passionately on her mouth. Her hands went around his neck and held him so tight he feared he wouldn't catch his breath. Sometime later he released her, letting her slide down him. Her eyes were like liquid chocolate as she looked up at him as if he was the most magnificent person she'd ever seen. He would work to keep that look there for the rest of his life.

"I love you with all my heart, Lauren. I promise you I'll always love you and Shawn."

She cupped his cheek. "That's all I'll ever need.

Wherever you go, I'll go." Coming up on her toes, she kissed him.

After they broke apart she asked, "So what's all this packing about? Where're you moving to? Another part of town?"

He grinned. "Actually, I'm hoping to start a new practice in a small Oklahoma town. I was waiting to see if the nurse there would forgive me for being such a jerk." He looked into her eyes. "For not telling her that she is my life."

The joy was evident in her eyes before she gave him a kiss that let him know she felt the same about him.

She pulled away. "So you're moving to Last Stop?"

"Only if you agree to marry me, honeymoon with me in Venice, let me be a father to Shawn and any other children we might have."

"I can't think of anything more wonderful." She kissed him again then gave him a serious look. "I'll move to Boston, if that's what you want."

"You said I belonged here but you're wrong. I belong with you. With *Shawn*. Wherever you are is my home. Where I find happiness."

* * * * *

LET'S TALK

Romance

For exclusive extracts, competitions
and special offers, find us online:

f facebook.com/millsandboon

◎ @millsandboonuk

🐦 @millsandboon

Or get in touch on 0844 844 1351*

For all the latest titles coming soon,
visit millsandboon.co.uk/nextmonth

Want even more
ROMANCE?

Join our bookclub today!

'Mills & Boon books, the perfect way to escape for an hour or so.'

Miss W. Dyer

'Excellent service, promptly delivered and very good subscription choices.'

Miss A. Pearson

'You get fantastic special offers and the chance to get books before they hit the shops'

Mrs V. Hall

Visit millsandbook.co.uk/Bookclub and save on brand new books.

MILLS & BOON